D1501623

The Soldier's Secret

Heather Osborne

This is a work of fiction. Names, characters, places, and incidents are either the product of the author's imagination or used fictitiously and any resemblance to actual people, alive or dead, business, establishments, locales, or events is entirely coincidental.
Any reference to real events, businesses, or organizations is intended to give the fiction a sense of realism and authenticity.

All errors are the sole responsibility of the author.

Cover Design by Victoria Cooper Art

Edited by Susie Watson

Hardcover ISBN: 9798507219087

Paperback ISBN: 978-1505987720

Dedication and Acknowledgements

This book is dedicated to my father, David, a historical re-enactor with The American Civil War Association in California. Thank you for inspiring my love of history.

Kind thanks to Scott Davis for his prolific knowledge about the American Civil War.

Author's Note

I have done my very best to portray conditions during the American Civil War to the height of my abilities. I would like to remind the reader while this is based on historical events, it is a complete work of fiction. I have taken a few creative liberties with some of the details.

Thank you for reading, and enjoy "The Soldier's Secret."

Prologue

December, 1862
Fredericksburg, Virginia

"You have to hold him tighter!" The Union doctor showed no sympathy at all for the man writhing in blood on his table.

"Yes, Sir!" The youth compressed all his strength on the man, turning his face away from the bloody limb, which vaguely resembled a leg.

The sawbones grasped the bone saw firmly and without much ado, began vigorously amputating the man's leg. The strangled screams echoed in the youth's ears and he swallowed hard to prevent himself from losing what little food he had in his belly.

The soldier passed out as soon as the doctor hit bone. Although it seemed to take an eternity, the whole procedure was over in ten minutes. The youth crawled off the man and waited while the doctor stitched the wound. Leaving a hole for drainage, he bandaged what was left of the man's lower right leg.

"Get him moved!" The doctor was already preparing for the subsequent amputation. The youth followed the stretcher out of the tent, ignoring the cries of the next soldier. He wanted to slam his hands over his ears and fuse his eyes closed.

The carnage was almost too much to bear. The Confederate Army had devastated the Army of the Potomac. The youth hung his head and trudged along, scuffing his boot in the dirt. A hand grabbed his ankle and he steadied himself.

"Water...gimme water, boy." The soldier was on a stretcher awaiting the surgeon, with a gaping hole in his abdomen, intestines spilling out.

The youth knelt down and wiped away some dirt from the man's face, "Won't be long now."

The soldier fished in his pocket and pressed a gold watch into the youth's hand. "My boy...he'll be 10...man of the house now...take this to him. Name's on the inside." He grabbed the youth's collar, "Promise me, boy."

Folding his fingers around the watch, the youth quickly nodded and the man collapsed back, his eyes vacant. Rocking back on his heels, he stared for a few moments at the dead man. Nearby, soldiers were digging a mass grave for the men who had fallen on the battlefield. Removing his kepi, he said a short prayer and made the sign of the cross before rising and shuffling his way to the hospital tent.

Two officers were speaking in hushed tones and barely noticed the thin youth entering the canvas tent. The smell of death permeated the air, along with urine and vomit. The surviving patients were awaiting transport to the city from the battlefield. The youth quickly located his compatriot and pulled a wooden stool to the side of his cot.

"Water..."

The youth placed his hand on the man's chest, "You cannot have any yet, William. Soon though. They are going to take you into the city."

Will gave him a weak smile and grasped the narrow-boned hand, "If I survive long..."

"You will! Have faith."

"Hurts like hellfire, Em. Wish we were back at home. It'll be Christmas soon...I wish I could taste my ma's cookin' one last time..." William let out a sigh and shut his eyes again.

Hanging his head, the youth angrily brushed away a tear, speaking in a voice low enough for Will not to hear, "Me too, Will. Me too..."

1

Rochester, New York
July, 1861

William Mansfield burst through the door of his mother's brownstone home waving a copy of *The New York Times*, "McDowell was defeated at Manassas!"

His mother and sister departed the parlor at the same time his father and brother exited the study. William Mansfield Sr. took the newspaper out of his son's hand and skimmed the article plastered on the front page, "It's not possible!"

Gathering close to his shoulders, all read the sparse article as Will paced back and forth restlessly across the foyer. Emma Mansfield watched her elder brother with some apprehension before turning her face to her father, "What does it mean?"

William Sr. folded the paper and addressed his daughter, "It means, my dear daughter, this war is going to go on much longer than any of us could possibly anticipate."

Harrison, the youngest of the siblings and not yet sixteen, carried the passionate nature of a boy on the cusp of manhood. "We need to enlist and fight! Defend the country from the Rebels!"

Will faced him, a grave expression on his handsome face, "No, Harrison. You have to go to college and get educated. Learn the business from Father and carry on the family name." Their father owned a general store in the neighborhood, catering to the upper-class populace. He made a healthy living for his family selling his wares.

Harrison scowled and his father clapped a hand on his shoulder, "Your brother is right. You are too young to enlist anyways."

Rosemarie Mansfield clasped her hands together, fighting tears. Her children were so headstrong, she knew she could never rid Will of his desire to go off and fight. William Sr. placed a consoling arm around his wife. It amazed him she had borne three intelligent children to him, being a wisp of a woman herself. Still, her emerald eyes sparkled as brightly as they did the first moment he laid eyes on her at a country social. He smiled to himself remembering when he released her wavy, auburn hair from the pins on their wedding night.

"There, there, Rose. Will has a good head on his shoulders. If he chooses to fight for a cause, we must support him. Harrison will be safe here, won't you, boy?" He subtly urged his son to reassure his distressed mother.

"Sure, Mother, I'll stay." His disappointment was evident as he slumped his shoulders forward.

Emma gazed up at her eldest brother, "So, you will go to defend the country?"

Will nodded, "It's our patriotic duty, Sis."

"And what is my patriotic duty?" Her brow furrowed.

Her father stepped in, "Your duty, Emma, is to marry a man who will provide for you and to raise children. Not to be bothered with this godforsaken war."

"William!" Rose often took Emma along with her to the abolitionist meetings. She did not want to resign her only daughter to a simple family life.

Frowning, William took his eldest son by the arm. "Come. If you're going to fight, we may as well get your enlistment over with. You'll need money and supplies. Harrison, you can come too."

Harrison hung his head and followed the men out of the house, the door slamming behind them, leaving the house in deafening silence. Rose reached out to her daughter, who stood facing the wall, arms crossed in defiance.

"Emma, you must believe your father did not mean to say you should do nothing with your life."

Emma turned, meeting her mother's gaze with the same stunning green eyes, "Why should women have to stay and care for the home while men go off and fight?"

"We fight our own battles here. Come. We best go see Mrs. Hastings. She will tell us if the Ladies' Society has begun any war efforts. With luck, this will all be over soon and our dear William will never see the battlefield."

Mrs. Elizabeth Hastings was the most well-known lady of the neighborhood. In order to be accepted by the close-knit society, one required the nod of her carefully coiffed head. She took immediately to the young Mansfield family, especially the daughter, Emma, who she saw as having high aspirations beyond the duties of wife and mother. Mrs. Hastings' husband had passed away fighting in the War of 1812, leaving her a young widow. She never remarried and had no children. Her husband left her a sizeable inheritance, allowing her to live comfortably in an elaborate brownstone a few doors down from the Mansfield's.

Mrs. Hastings wore the garb of a widow and would not be swayed to give up her black, silk dress. She wore a cameo pin at her high collar, and her white hair was pulled back in a severe bun sans the ringlets common with other ladies her age. Even in the warm summer months, she would not be seen in anything less. The color was in stark contrast to the cotton lawn Emma and her mother wore to keep cool. She rose as her only servant, a freed black woman called Millie, showed the ladies into the parlor.

"Ah! Good afternoon Rosemarie and Emma. How kind of you to pay me a visit on this lovely day!" Mrs. Hastings kissed both their cheeks and gestured for them to sit. "May I offer you some lemonade and butter cake? Millie has made it fresh."

Rose smiled graciously and perched on the edge of a floral suite. "Yes, a drink would be refreshing, thank you."

Mrs. Hastings smiled dotingly at Emma, "Tell me, how are your studies, my dear?"

"Very well, ma'am. My father was discussing sending me away to school, but with the war, I fear it will be impossible now."

"Tut tut, never fear, Emma, darling. We need strong, educated women here." She glanced at Rose, "And I assume you have come to ask about any prospective war efforts? I did see your husband and sons heading in the direction of the recruitment office earlier."

Rose nodded, pausing to allow Millie to serve the refreshments, "Yes, Mrs. Hastings. I believe we should prepare for the worst. The heads of our country seem to have underestimated the Confederacy." She said the word as if it were a rotten piece of meat.

"Now, my dear, we must understand it will be hard for the women there as well." Mrs. Hastings believed everyone, man and woman, should be aware of the political climate. Ignorance was not bliss.

Emma sipped her lemonade in silence as her elders discussed what needed to be done. They decided a drive to gather old linens for bandages would be the best way to start, as well as sewing cold weather clothing. Winter would be arriving sooner, rather than later. The sun was dipping in the sky by the time Emma and her mother emerged from the house. Mrs. Hastings urged them to come by the following evening. She would be hosting another abolitionist meeting with a guest speaker. Rose assured her they would be there.

Emma looped her arm through her mother's as they walked along the sidewalk. Rose nodded politely to neighbors as they passed, the people taking advantage of the balmy, evening air. Upon arriving home, they were greeted with shouts.

"I do not see how it's fair! William is only three years older than me! What difference does three years make?" Harrison was still arguing he should be allowed to go, "I could be in the regimental band or a flag bearer! Those are more than respectable positions."

"Either of which puts you directly in the line of fire. Do not assume I am ignorant to war, boy." William Sr.'s voice was low, but firm.

Rose scurried down the hall and burst into the study, "If you dare go off to war, Harrison Gray Mansfield, you will break your poor mother's heart!"

The room grew silent as Rose collapsed into her daughter's arms, sobbing.

Harrison scuffed his boot on the carpet and stomped from the room. His bedroom door banged shut.

"Rose, my love, do not upset yourself. I will see myself off to war before I let them have Harrison." He drew her from Emma's grasp into his own. Emma quietly withdrew, making her way up the stairs, listening to her father murmur reassurances and endearments to her mother. She passed William's open door and paused. He was dressed in full regalia, brass buttons glinting in the candlelight.

Emma leaned against the door frame in a most unladylike fashion, "You are really going to fight, Will?"

He turned and she was able to see all his finery. "Yes, it's my duty. James and Martin have already enlisted. They were there when Father and I arrived." James and Martin Clark were twin brothers and Will's best friends, "We've been assigned to the same regiment."

Emma fiddled with the sleeve of her dress, "When do you leave?"

"The week after next we go to basic training. We will learn to use rifles, cook, and keep ourselves fit."

Emma did not bother to point out he sounded like a recruitment advertisement in the paper, "What about Bridget? Have you told her?"

Will stopped straightening his uniform jacket, a muscle in his jaw twitching at the mention of his sweetheart, "She'll find out soon enough, I suppose. Her brother was there today as well."

"If I were you, and this is the opinion of a humble woman, I would hightail your behind over there and beg her forgiveness for not being up front. It's the least she deserves." Emma glowered at her elder sibling, "Because if you do not, William Mansfield, I shall think you the most despicable man who ever walked this earth!"

Will's ears turned red, "Aww, Emma...I suppose I didn't think of it that way."

She poked him in the chest, square between the buttons of his uniform, "Bridget is the sweetest, kindest girl in all the neighborhood."

"I know, Emma, I know. I'm going!" He did not even bother to change as he trotted down the stairs and out the door. Emma watched from the upstairs window as he crossed the street to the Nelson house.

Bridget Nelson lived with her father and older brother, their mother having passed away shortly after her birth. Will apprehensively knocked on the door. Bridget opened it briefly, before slamming it back in his face.

"Damn." Will muttered before knocking again and pleading, "Bridget, please. Hear me out."

Bridget cracked the door open again. Her fine, blonde hair was askew, tendrils escaping from the carefully pleated knot at the nape of her neck. Sky blue eyes were red from crying. Will did not give her a chance to shut the door on him again and pushed it open. She stepped back, dabbing her eyes with a lace handkerchief.

"Bridget..." He swallowed hard as the shadow of her father fell over the pair.

Clement Nelson observed the pair for a few moments before speaking, "So, William, I hear from Nathanial you are off to war as well."

"Yes, sir."

"Well, safe travels to you, son." Mr. Nelson held out his hand and Will shook it, grateful he was not being held at gunpoint, "You two may have the leave of the parlor. I suspect you have some explaining to do." He winked at Will, and disappeared into the kitchen.

Bridget turned in a dramatic huff, very unlike her, and stormed into the parlor. Will followed, looking rather sheepish. He opened his mouth to speak, and was quickly assaulted with words.

"William Mansfield, you are despicable!"

Will could barely contain a chuckle. Bridget glared at him and he suppressed it, making his excuses, "That's what Emma said you would say."

"Were you going to run off at a hot trot to war, without even speaking to me?" She collapsed into one of the high back armchairs.

Will quickly knelt before her, "No, Bridget, never." He fumbled for her hand and brought it to his lips.

Bridget's lower lip trembled, "What if you die and I never see you again?"

"Oh, sweetheart, nothing could keep me from coming back to you." He ran a hand through his dark red hair and sat back on his heels.

Bridget sniffled, "How can you be sure?"

It was a question Will could not answer. He paused in thought and then stood, "Bridget, wait here." He quickly left the parlor, returning after a few minutes. This time, Will dropped to one knee, "Bridget, will you marry me? Give me a reason to come back from this war."

Bridget began to cry harder and Will embraced her softly. She nodded and clung to him, "Yes, you fool-hearted man, I will marry you."

The joyous news overshadowed the impending departure of many of the young men of the neighborhood. The celebration was bittersweet, but it gave many hope for the future. A special church service took place on the following Sunday to pray for the safe return of the men, and to bless Will and Bridget's union. As it was more practical, Bridget would remain at her father's home until Will returned. She clung to Emma's hand, happy to have a sister. Emma promised to visit often, urging her to pay call to them as well.

William and Rose supported their son's impulsive decision, each hoping Will would live to come home and raise a family. Tears flowed freely as the following week passed in a blur. Harrison stood stone-faced as his brother went off to fight a battle he could never have any part of. Emma comforted her mother in those quiet hours following the departure, as her father stood stoic. All jubilation ended and reality soon sunk in.

Rochester, New York
December, 1861

Dearest Bridget,

I hope this letter finds you well. We are traveling down the Southern coastline and now under the command of Major General McClellan, whom you have no doubt read about in the local papers. The plantation owners are feeling the pressure. Clouds of smoke billow over their crop fields as they burn the cotton.

Is your pregnancy progressing well? Imagine my surprise to hear I was to be a father so soon after our marriage. I insist you stay with my mother and sister as your time draws near. It will bring me great comfort.

Not much else to write as I do not want to distress you. My hopes of being home for a visit at Christmas have been dismissed as there is no way to retreat out of this hellhole, excuse the language.

All my love to you,
Will

Bridget read the letter to Emma and Rose as they sat in the parlor before a roaring fire, each trying not to think of Will shivering in the cold outdoors warmed only by a meager campfire. It was a shock to everyone Bridget fell pregnant so quickly. She carried her pregnancy well, and the doctor was expecting the baby to arrive in late April. All three women worked hard stitching clothing for the fighting men, as well as knitting the occasional baby garment. Rose was pleased as punch to be a grandmother.

New York had yet to see some of the strains of war already evident in the lower states closer to the Confederacy. The newspaper brought sparse bits of news. Great Britain was not supporting the war and had placed embargoes on the states. A great victory was won in Congress, as Mrs. Hastings read out slavery was to be abolished in the nation's capital and fugitive slaves would not be forced to return to the South. Men continued to volunteer for the Union Army. The neighborhood saw more and more of their young men marching off in uniform.

Bridget ran her hand over her distended abdomen, "I should like a girl. That way, I never have to watch her go off to battle."

Rose nodded sympathetically, patting Emma's hand, "It is such a comfort to have Emma by my side. Harrison broods day and night. He says he hopes the war lasts until he turns eighteen and can go fight."

Emma concentrated on her sewing and listened to her mother and sister-in-law chatter about names. No matter how hard she worked with the Ladies' Society, Emma still felt inadequate. She stood and gathered her wool shawl from the back of the chair, "I think I am going to take a little walk."

Rose glanced out the window, "Very well. Be careful and come in if you become too cold. I do not need you getting ill."

Emma smiled, "I will." She gave Bridget's abdomen a

loving pat and exited into the brisk, winter air. Slowly making her way down the street, she ended up at her father's store. Pushing open the door caused the little bell to sound, and her father came out from the back, smiling at the sight of his daughter.

"Emma, what are you doing out in this weather? I would have thought you would be home in the parlor." He dusted some flour off his hands.

Emma circled around the shop, touching a bolt of fabric here, a leather-bound journal there. "I needed a break from ladies' pursuits."

William straightened his apron and contemplated his daughter. "I have been meaning to apologize to you for what I said before Will left..."

"What do you mean, Papa?" Emma paused in her rounds.

"You are meant for stronger stuff, and I will be proud no matter what you choose to do. I wish we could have sent you away to be educated..." Her father looked ashamed for the first time in his life.

"Oh, Papa, please do not be upset." Emma moved to him and hugged him, "I am satisfied to do my work for the Ladies' Society. When the hospital is up and running, I am going to volunteer there as a nurse. I promise, you have not let me down."

William held his daughter at arm's length, "You are so charitable. I could not be more proud of you, Emma." He moved to a shelf and straightened some stock, "How is Harrison?"

Emma chewed her lower lip in contemplation, trying to find the best words so as not to hurt her father's feelings, "He..."

Smiling knowingly, her father sighed, "There is no need to try and sugarcoat the truth, Emma. I know he is still upset at me. That boy is too impulsive."

"I feel as if he does not even care to fight for a cause. He wants to prove himself a man. I do not know how killing someone else makes you a man." Emma wrapped her shawl tighter around her shoulders, a chill shooting through her body, despite the shop's warmth.

William placed a hand on either side of Emma's face, "Do not fret. I will speak to him when we arrive home. If you wait, I can take us in the carriage." He gave her cheek a final pat and went into the back.

Emma settled herself on the stool behind the desk and picked up a copy of *Uncle Tom's Cabin*, flipping to a familiar chapter. She read for several minutes when a crash followed by a cry of pain startled her. Jumping up, she ran to the back stock room and found her father on the floor, his leg stuck under a large crate. His face was white.

"Papa!" Emma rushed to his side.

William's fists were clenched. "Fetch the doctor, Emma. Quickly. Mr. Henderson as well."

Emma raced from the store and darted across the street to the blacksmith. She shouted at him over the clang of his hammer, "Mr. Henderson!"

Henderson stopped and wiped his hands. He was a stocky man with strong arms from pounding metal fittings. "Emma! What is it?"

"My father, sir. A crate has fallen on his leg! Come quickly, please! I must fetch the doctor!" She hurried off down the street.

Henderson removed his thick leather apron, and jogged over to the store.

Emma reached the doctor's office at the end of the street. She pounded on the door with her fist, calling out.

Doctor Colin McCafferty opened the door to receive the distraught female into his office. He quickly recognized her, waiting a few moments for her to gain her composure before inquiring as to the nature of her affliction.

"My father, Doctor McCafferty. A crate fell on his leg at the shop. I fear he is badly hurt." Emma grabbed his hand

and pulled him to the door, “Please! You must come quickly!”

Colin felt his heart lurch at the soft-touch of her hand, but maintained his business-like demeanor. He retrieved his coat and bag from the desk, and hurried after Emma back to the shop. Henderson was already in the back stock room. He had lifted the crate from her father’s leg, which was twisted at an odd angle.

Emma moved and knelt by her father, taking his hand in her own. Colin surveyed the scene and turned to Henderson. “I will have to set the leg before I can move him. Do you have any strong whiskey?”

Henderson nodded and withdrew a flask from his pocket, passing it to William. Emma knew her father hardly ever imbibed in spirits and the brew would do quick work. Colin fixed his gaze on Emma. “You must hold him.”

Emma wrapped her arms around her father’s shoulders. Colin turned to Henderson and gestured to William’s thigh. “Place your hands here and, on the count of three, pull hard and firmly.”

The procedure was over in seconds, William’s strangled scream piercing the air. He did not pass out though. The doctor made a temporary splint, and they transported him back to the Mansfield residence. Rose made way for the men as they swiftly bore William up to the bedroom. She assisted them in dressing him into his nightshirt. Doctor McCafferty instructed her in the care of the leg, and made a sturdier support for the broken bone. It was a clean break and would heal in about six weeks.

Emma was sitting in the parlor alone, waiting for the house to settle down. Her mother thanked Mr. Henderson and the doctor profusely, before insisting they stay for dinner. Mr. Henderson politely declined as he had to return to his fires and make sure they were properly stoked before heading home, but the doctor accepted the invitation heartily, not wishing to dine alone for another night.

Rose informed the cook there would be an extra guest for dinner. She ushered him into the parlor to wait for the meal to be prepared, while she went to check on her husband, begging the good doctor's indulgence.

Colin smiled kindly and entered the room, warmed immediately by the fire, and by the presence of Emma Mansfield. He often saw her coming and going from her father's store, admiring her beauty from afar. He wasn't ashamed to admit he knew every move of her skirt, and how each lock of her auburn hair fell on her neck. What he lacked was the courage to ask her to walk with him after church on a Sunday, or attend one of the local social often held by the society women.

"Miss Mansfield." He cleared his throat softly.

Emma drew her gaze away from the flickering flames. Her eyes were red from crying. She sniffled in a much-undignified manner, before identifying the guest. "How is my father, Doctor?"

Colin motioned to an empty seat and she nodded. He sat across from her with a reassuring smile. "With rest, he will recover quickly. I sense he is a headstrong man. You and your mother must make sure he stays in bed as long as possible."

The doctor's features were expressive, but there was no hint of deception in his kind voice. Doctor McCafferty had come to their town fresh out of medical school and extensive studies abroad. He was young, but this did not stop the citizens from flocking to his small practice. He kept himself informed on the latest medical procedures. In addition, he was a highly desirable bachelor with his easy smile and gentle touch, not to mention his handsome countenance. His face accented by carelessly combed brown hair and alert eyes, which shifted from green to blue in the light.

"We will do our best to make sure of that, Doctor."

"Pardon me for asking, but who will run the store for your father? Certainly in times like these, it would not be wise to close up?" Colin stretched out his legs and crossed them at the ankles. He did not mean to sound impudent or rude, but was merely trying to hear a few more words from the rosy lips of his companion.

Emma turned back to him, well aware of the smoldering gaze of his aquamarine eyes. She blushed, but continued with polite conversation, "My mother and I will no doubt assist in the store. My youngest brother, Harrison, will help as well, I'm sure. Thank you for your concern."

"And how is your eldest brother, Miss Mansfield? I was recently checking in on his wife. She seems to be in good health, and her condition is progressing nicely."

"He is well. We last heard from him this morning. It seems the army is marching down the Southern coastline. Are you not going to enlist, sir? I am sure they are in need of good doctors."

Colin cleared his throat, "Ah, well, I have considered it, but my patients need me here. I suppose if things were to get worse, I would happily offer my services to the Union Army."

Emma nodded and the room descended into silence aside from the occasional pop of the fire. The lapse in conversation gave Colin ample time to study Emma's profile in the dim light. Something stirred deep in his chest, as he let his eyes wander over the curve of her neck and the stray ringlets lingering there. Before he could stop, the words tumbled from his mouth.

"Ms. Mansfield, would you accompany me to the Christmas fundraiser social the Ladies' Society is hosting this Saturday next?"

Startled by the sudden outburst, Emma jumped slightly, "Oh! Well, I..."

Colin sat forward on his seat, "I will, of course, understand if you already have an escort."

Emma rewarded him with a giggle and a soft upward curve of her lips. "Doctor McCafferty, I do not have an escort, and I would very much like to accompany you."

Rose entered the parlor, after eavesdropping at the door. She was pleased the doctor had taken an interest in her daughter. He was a good man, with a stable profession and well-respected in the community. Colin immediately rose when she came through the portal. Emma placed her hand over her mouth, stifling a giggle at his eagerness to please.

"The meal is ready, Doctor. If you would follow me. I ordered a tray to be taken up to my husband. He is resting comfortably thanks to your efforts."

"I am glad to hear, ma'am." He flushed a bit as he followed the ladies into the dining room.

"Emma, will you fetch your brother, please? I am disappointed he did not come down when he heard your father being brought in. I assume he is still upset." Rose allowed the doctor to pull out her chair.

Ascending the stairs, Emma left their presence. Rose turned her attention to Colin while they were served a rich beef broth and pieces of crusty bread. "Tell me, Doctor, how did you come to our part of the world?"

Colin took a drink of the served wine, and placed his napkin in his lap, "I grew up in Maine, where my father worked in the logging industry. He became quite prosperous and was able to send me to study in England. My mother passed away in child birth, and my father never remarried. I grew up an only child."

Rose delicately sipped her soup as she listened. "How tragic for your father. Her death must have impacted him deeply."

Colin nodded in agreement, as he ate in between conversation. "Yes, it was. Pardon me, Mrs. Mansfield, but your daughter seems to have been absent for an extended period of time. Would you permit me to go fetch her?"

Setting her spoon down, Rose smiled knowingly, "Do you admire my daughter, sir?"

Colin coughed, "Excuse me?"

"There is no shame in it. She is a lovely and accomplished

woman. I do approve of you courting her, since my husband is not well enough to be asked."

Colin pushed his chair back and inclined his head, "Thank you, ma'am. If you will excuse me, I will see what is keeping Miss Mansfield."

Emma rapped several times on her brother's door, eventually turning the knob and admitting herself into Harrison's room. The window was wide open, allowing in flurries of chilled wind. She hurried over and shut it, before surveying the surroundings. Harrison's wardrobe was open and items of clothing were missing. The realization slowly dawned: her youngest brother had fled the family home. She frantically searched his desk, finally discovering a single piece of paper on his pillow.

All I wanted was to fight for a cause. It seems since the Union Army will not have me, I will have to fight for another.

My love to Mother and Emma.

The paper slipped from her fingers to the floor. Her father was in no state to receive such news. She slumped onto the bed and closed her eyes, letting the tears flow freely. How could Harrison be so careless and so stubborn as to abandon his family and go fight for the opposing army, the men who were probably, at this moment, shooting at his brother? She barely acknowledged Colin coming into the room.

"Emma?" He addressed her informally upon seeing her state. "What is it? Should I fetch your mother?"

Emma wiped her eyes, "No, not yet. Could you sit with me for a while?"

Spotting the paper at her feet, Colin surmised what had happened with little prompting. He quietly sat next to her on the bed, and held her while she wept for her broken family.

They eventually descended from Harrison's room and broke the news to her mother that Harrison had ran away to parts unknown. Rose fell into a swoon and the doctor carried her to bed. He prescribed a sleeping draught for her and checked on William. Emma managed to explain to her father what had happened, showing him the letter.

"Damn that boy! Doesn't he understand this makes him a traitor? He could be jailed, or worse!" William struggled to sit up.

"Mr. Mansfield, you must not exert yourself. The leg must heal." The doctor pressed a firm hand to the man's shoulder.

Emma gently touched Colin's arm. "I will show you out, Doctor."

Knowing the family needed to be alone at this tragic time, Colin fetched his bag and allowed Emma to show him to the door. He faced her for a moment, "Emma, if you do need anything, please do not hesitate to come find me." Pressing his handkerchief in her hand, he smiled warmly, "For your tears."

Emma watched him disappear into the darkness, clutching the cloth to her breast.

Despite the family circumstances, Rose insisted Emma attend the social with Doctor McCafferty. Her daughter had been working herself ragged, keeping the store open and running while William was incapacitated. Bridget grinned broadly at her sister-in-law as they fitted her into the dress.

"You both really shouldn't have. Fabric is becoming scarce! When did you manage to do all this?" Emma admired her form in the mirror. The bodice of the emerald dress cut low across her shoulders, accented by delicate, black lace while the matching silk skirt flared out over her new lawn petticoat.

"Tosh! We worked as hard as you these last weeks!" Bridget hoisted herself to her feet, "It's our Christmas present to you. Who knows, it may catch you a doctor!"

Rose laughed. "Hush, Bridget! It's not proper to speak of such things."

Emma twirled in front of the mirror, "I think I will be the envy of all the ladies at the social. Is it wicked of me?"

"Nonsense, my sweet girl." Her mother held her at arm's length. The day maid had done some sort of magic and tamed her locks into an intricate mass of curls and twists, adorning it with matching pieces of lace. "Now, something is missing..." Rose left the room and returned with sparkling diamond and emerald earrings, along with a matching necklace.

"Oh, Mother! I cannot! I will lose them!" Emma backed up a step.

Rose's face softened. "Emma, my darling daughter, please. It would bring me great joy to see them out. As it would it your father!" She fastened them on without further complaint.

Bridget clapped her hands. "You are a vision, Emma! I wish I looked as lovely as you."

Emma cupped her new sister's cheek. "You glow, Bridget, and are far more beautiful than I!"

Rose took her hand, "Come. We must show your father before he tries to get himself out of bed!"

The trio of women burst into William's room, chattering loudly about the social. William chuckled and held up his hands. "Ladies! Can I see my daughter properly?"

Emma stepped forward and spun slowly before her father. His eyes lit up, and he inclined his head in approval. "If it were anyone else, but the good doctor you were going with, I may have cause to worry. Come give your father a kiss, child, and have a wonderful time."

She graciously bestowed a kiss on his cheek, knowing he was still deeply troubled by Harrison's departure. With finances as they were, there was no way he could pay a man to go after his youngest son and, even if he could, no one would risk crossing into enemy lines. There had been no word from him. Emma took her father's hand and gave it a squeeze before the bell sounded through the home. As quickly as they bustled into the room, the women left, leaving William laughing again.

Colin tucked a finger inside the collar of his dress shirt, it having become increasingly tighter during his short carriage ride to the Mansfield's residence. He watched Emma trudging daily to the store to keep the family going. Many times he had wanted to take the burden away from her. He hoped this evening would bring her some joy in the Christmas season, at least. The wrapped gift he had tucked into the carriage seat would bring it to a perfect end. Pressing the bell, Colin took a step back as the door was almost immediately thrown open by Bridget.

"Good evening, Doctor McCafferty." She bobbed a small curtsey.

"Mrs. Mansfield. I do recommend you not exert yourself so in your condition." All professional mannerisms were resumed, and he doffed his hat, as she allowed him into the home.

"The baby is fine, sir. He kicks me almost constantly!"

Colin turned to head up the stairs. "I should pay my respects to Mr. Mansfield..." He was abruptly pulled in the direction of the parlor.

"Oh, no, Papa Mansfield is asleep. He said to send you his good wishes. Emma is in the parlor." She gave him a gentle shove and giggled, clasping a hand over her mouth.

The parlor door swung open, and Rose emerged. "Good evening, Doctor McCafferty. I trust you are well? You look rather pale."

Clearing his throat, Colin shifted on his feet. "I am well, Mrs. Mansfield. Thank you for asking. I hear Mr. Mansfield is doing better? I will be back later in the week to check on him."

"Very good, Doctor. Emma is waiting for you." She gave his arm a reassuring pat and whispered, "You will be fine." Withdrawing, she ushered an open-mouthed, protesting Bridget to the kitchen.

Hesitating at the door, Colin drew in a steadying breath. Upon crossing the thresh-hold, the object of his affections came into view, standing in the gentle glow of the firelight. Her positioning afforded him the greatest view of her new frock which seemed to accentuate every curve of her womanly form. He cleared his throat delicately. "Good evening, Miss Mansfield."

Emma turned, and Colin's heart nearly stopped. Most certainly she was a vision before, but this was an entirely new and thrilling woman who stood before him. In a momentary lapse, he cursed himself for not inviting Emma to a formal event sooner. She dipped low into a curtsey, "Doctor McCafferty. You are quite handsome this evening."

Colin stepped forward and drew one of her gloved hands into his own, gracing it with a kiss, "And you are a delight to behold."

Her lips curving into a smile, Emma felt her cheeks warm again. The doctor cleaned up exceptionally well, and was wearing a dark suit, accenting his broad shoulders and tapering at the waist. "Shall we go? I hope you do not mind. I was asked by Mrs. Hastings to assist with some of the baked goods for the auction."

Searching the room briefly, he retrieved her delicate lace shawl, draping it over her shoulders, taking advantage of the closeness to brush his warm fingertips over her shoulders. "I do not mind at all, Miss Mansfield."

At the door, the doctor retrieved her woolen cape from one of the house servants and performed the same ritual. By this time, Emma was so flushed by the subtle gestures the cool evening air did not seem to bother her in the slightest. Colin assisted her into the carriage and took his place next to her, urging the single gelding onward to their destination.

Rose smiled from the window, arms crossed over her body. William observed his wife in quiet thought. "What is it, my dear?"

Turning and going to sit at her husband's side, she took his hand in hers, "I was recalling our first social. What a delightful time Emma will have."

"Small blessings in the midst of chaos." William drew his wife close for a kiss.

The hall was bustling by the time Colin stabled the horse and lifted Emma from the carriage seat, leaving the horses to the care of the stable boy. Their journey had passed in relative silence, each enjoying the quiet evening air, as well as the tinkling sound of the bells attached to the horse's halter. It was unusual not to see their little part of the town draped in snow flurries, as was common for the time of year. Colin even briefly commented on the fact. Emma was glad of it. Maybe if the weather here was so agreeable, her brother would not be suffering so much.

Handing his coat and hat off to one of the servants engaged for the evening, Colin removed Emma's cape and drew her arm through his. She could feel several of the young ladies present shooting daggers her way. Emma knew it was no secret several had tried to entice the doctor to invite them to this affair, and would do anything to be in her position. She almost felt ashamed for thinking of ways to beg off helping with the auction so she could remain by his side for the evening.

The room was lavishly decorated with evergreen and holly. Mrs. Hastings oversaw everything personally and no expense was spared. There were a few remaining men in uniform who were heading out after the Christmas holidays. Colin led Emma over to the amply set buffet table, and scooped up a crystal glass of rum punch for each of them.

Leaning close, Colin murmured into her ear, "It has been a long time since I have been to a social."

Emma smiled up at him, and his form visibly relaxed, "I believe I have more cause to be nervous than you, Doctor."

He drew her to the side of the room and lowered his head, eyes twinkling, "Oh?"

Rising on tiptoe, Emma whispered into his ear, "I do believe there are at least four women over there who want to scratch my eyes out for coming with you."

The quartette of women comprised of Emma's former schoolmates, each insanely jealous of Emma's beauty and educational talent. Colin surveyed them with little interest.

"Ah yes. I do believe I recognize a few of them, one of whom was in my office earlier this week complaining of a pain in her leg."

Emma giggled prettily, hiding her mouth behind a gloved hand, "Oh my! I do hope she is sufficiently recovered?"

Colin winked, his eyes sparkling with mirth, "Oh, I would say she is quite recovered with the way she is stamping her foot."

Mrs. Hastings took the exact moment to bustle over to the striking couple. "Ah, Emma darling! You are stunning! I trust this is the dress your mother was telling me about?" She held the girl at arm's length, "Yes, it does suit you and brings out the color in your eyes." Turning to the doctor, she continued in her compliments, "And my, my! You managed to coax the dear doctor from his office! How lovely to see you again, Doctor McCafferty."

Colin afforded her a deep bow, "It is my pleasure to be escorting Miss Mansfield this evening. I presume you are in good health, Mrs. Hastings?"

"Oh, tosh! I am as strong as an ox! Now, if some lovely couple would only open up the dancing? It seems our guests are quite static this evening." She gestured to the small band of musicians employed for the evening's festivities and they struck up a waltz.

Colin held his hand out to Emma, "Shall we?" He escorted her to the dance floor and effortlessly fell into the steps of the dance.

"You are full of surprises, Doctor." Emma beamed up at him as he spun her around.

He dipped his head, "Colin. Please."

Emma was struck breathless, and she felt slightly lightheaded. Whether her affliction was from the punch or Colin, she could not yet determine. The dance ended and they clapped politely along with the few other couples, who had joined them for the intimate dance. The troop threw in a few faster country dances, but it was the waltzes the attendees seemed to favor. Colin even managed to coax Mrs. Hastings out for a dance or two, while Emma attended to her duties for the society, much to the chagrin of her rivals. It was not for lack of trying. Colin had to fend off some of the more ardent ladies, as the punch took hold of them and drove them to boldness.

The evening drew to a close, and the attendees trickled out of the hall. It was nearly one o'clock in the morning and Emma struggled to suppress yawns with her gloved hand. Colin agilely placed her into the carriage and they began the short journey back to the Mansfield residence. Snow began to float down from the sky, powdering the ground with white flecks. Without intending to, Emma rested her head on Colin's broad shoulder, her eyes closing as the motion of the carriage lulled her to sleep.

Colin watched the auburn head now perched on his shoulder and he felt a blossoming in his chest. All the shyness melted away and he hoped this was the beginning of something wonderful. They arrived before the house, and he reined the horse delicately as not to wake his companion, enjoying those few moments he had before relinquishing her back to her family.

Emma stirred and blinked. She cursed herself for falling asleep and murmured her apologies. Rising from her comfortable position, she blushed vivid scarlet as she noticed Colin had been watching her.

"Shush," he said before she could speak and dipped his head, brushing his lips over hers.

Freezing for a moment, Emma was shocked by the kiss, but did not stop Colin. She enjoyed the warm feeling spread through her body and the slight racing of her heart.

"I have something for you." Emma was disappointed the kiss ended, but curious to see what he had for her.

Withdrawing the wrapped parcel from beneath the seat, Colin handed it to her with a mischievous smile, "Open it."

Emma tore off the wrapping. Inside the parcel was a book, engraved in gold leaf. She read the title, "*Great Expectations* by Charles Dickens."

"I remember seeing you read in the shop window. I hope you do not have this one in your collection."

Wrapping her arms around him, Emma kissed him soundly on the cheek, "No! I do not! How kind of you, Colin. This must have cost a fortune!"

Colin flushed at the onslaught of affection, but was pleased beyond all reason she loved the gift. "I gave it some thought, and I did not take you for someone who would be as pleased by mere baubles and trinkets."

Emma cradled the book in her hand, tracing the embellishments, "No, Colin, you read me perfectly."

He circled the carriage to help her from the conveyance, "I know this is rather sudden, but would you permit me to call on you after church tomorrow?"

Emma accepted his assistance, giving his hand a momentary squeeze, "That would be lovely." Impulsively, she rose up and kissed him again, but he was not willing to accept another feathery touch on his lips. He slanted his mouth over hers and pulled her close for a long, ardent embrace, leaving Emma with the taste of him on her lips long after they parted company.

The Christmas season was met with sadness and joy. The Mansfield Family felt the absence of their beloved sons and brothers. Bridget missed her husband terribly and was struggling to cope with him being absent for so long. Letters were little consolation to her, but at least as long as the letters arrived, she knew Will was still with them. Rose insisted on inviting Doctor McCafferty to share in their celebration, since the subsequent snows prevented him from making a journey home. Bridget's father was also welcomed into the home. He considered it a great reprieve from his work at the bank.

Christmas Eve was spent in jovial celebration. Colin assisted in helping William from bed to join them in the parlor for the singing of carols and present exchanging. Emma shyly presented her new beau with a pair of sheepskin-lined gloves. There was much 'oohing' over the small baby garments Rose presented to her daughter-in-law. Everyone was satisfied with their gifts and retired upstairs after plum pudding. Rose insisted Colin take the guest bedroom, and he readily accepted the invitation.

Emma and Colin remained in the parlor after the rest of the family departed. William remarked to his wife he was pleased with the match, and hoped it would develop into more over the coming months. In an effort to maintain propriety, Colin stayed seated opposite Emma, observing her silently, as he was wont to do.

"I do miss them, Colin. I wish time would pass quickly." Emma's cheeks glowed from the warmth of the fire.

"Yes, I know you do. If I could bring them back for you safe and sound, I would." He meant it heartily.

She rewarded him for this sentiment with a smile, "I know you would. It is sweet of you to offer."

"I hope the New Year will bring more comforting news."

Emma shifted on the settee, wondering why he did not come closer to her. He had been a complete gentleman each time they had encountered each other. In truth, this was the first time they had been alone since the night of the social. She drew in a breath, and made a brave request, "Colin, will you come sit by me? There is a chill in the room."

"I thought you would never ask, my dear." Colin knew well there was no hint of cold air in the cozy parlor. He rose and settled next to her with a sigh.

Delicately placing a hand on his, Emma gazed upward to him, "Was it brazen of me?"

Turning his palm upward, Colin linked his fingers with hers, the contact of skin sending a shiver through Emma's body. "No, not at all. I believe if people want something in this world, life is too short not to ask for it."

Her lips curved into an impish smile, "If that is the case, I would much like you to kiss me again." Chaste pecks on the cheek after each departure left her wanting for something deeper.

Raising her hand to his lips, Colin placed a kiss on it, "Now, my dear lady, this is brazen." Releasing her hand, he placed his on the crook of her neck and drew her close, nuzzling her mouth with his.

Emma clung to his shoulders until she was breathless from his adoring affections. Her heart hammered in her chest and she wondered if she was falling in love with this dapper, intelligent man. Could he be falling in love with her? Emma's suspicions were soon affirmed when he abruptly broke the kiss.

"Emma, I cannot...I cannot go on like this!" He jumped to his feet and paced the room restlessly.

Emma was in shock, "Colin, whatever is the matter? Did I do something wrong?"

Colin fell to his knees by her side, "No, my darling, never. You could not possibly do anything wrong. I have been in love with you since the first moment I saw you. You occupy my every waking moment, and haunt my dreams. I know this is not the most opportune time, but will you marry me?"

Emma gasped and held a hand to her breast. He did love her! She bit her lower lip. "Oh, Colin...I...Yes! With my father's permission, yes!" She was laughing and crying at the same time and did not know how she was meant to feel. The tinkling chimes of the clock in the parlor signaled the hour had struck midnight.

"Merry Christmas, my sweet darling." Colin swept her into his arms for another ardent kiss.

Emma giggled and teasingly nipped his lip. "Merry Christmas indeed."

The New Year came and went with much excitement over the betrothal of Emma and Colin. Gossip swept like wildfire through their corner of the town as if there was something sinister about the engagement, but Mrs. Hastings, as always, put every rumor to rest with her staunch approval of the match. It was decided there would be a lengthy engagement, as Doctor McCafferty had not been called up by the Union Army to service the wounded on the battlefields.

By the end of January 1862, President Lincoln called for all the forces in training to begin their advance against the Confederates. Will sent a letter home vaguely detailing his training over the winter months. He reaffirmed to his family although he was exhausted, the war would be over soon. It seemed to be a constant theme among the news reports as well. As always, he sent his love to Bridget and the baby growing in her belly. He did not know when he would have leave, and the family began to suspect they would either never see him again, or see him once the war had ended.

William saw his leg healed by the end of January and resumed his duties at the store. No one, not even the doctor, could keep him from them. Emma accompanied him daily, assisting where she could. William insisted she take afternoons off to help with the Women's Society's war efforts as well as the planning of her wedding. Rose was frustrated the pair had not set a date, but with such uncertain times, she did not press them. Colin became a fixture in the household at meal times, and was always welcome.

A few weeks passed in much the same fashion, Emma and Colin's love only intensifying with the course of time. Finally, they announced the wedding would take place in August. The country was briefly in mourning, honoring the loss of President Lincoln's son. Bridget fretted at the news, worried her own child would succumb to such an illness. Colin was right there to reassure her he would see no such thing happen to the babe. It was a relief to have such a caring doctor close by.

Knowing her day was approaching, the family began to prepare for the birth of the baby, storing linens and towels for the event. The cradle, a gift from Will lovingly prepared and presented by Emma, already graced the room in which Bridget had taken up residence in the Mansfield home. Clement fretted over his daughter, and Rose was required to soothe him on more than one occasion with herbal teas. She admonished him for his worry and said women had been birthing babies for years.

March 5th, 1862

My dear Bridget,

Orders have been issued to advance. Cannot say where due to spies and regulations. All my love to you and the baby, which will soon be in your arms if I recollect correctly. Know I wish to be there more than anything. Cold and exhausted, but do not worry yourself. Much pleased to hear of Emma's engagement. Love to Mother, Father, and Emma. Cannot promise I will be home soon, but I pray for it.

Love, Will.

The short missive received in the morning post of March 15th sent Bridget into labor. Rose had suspected her time was nearing as the burden in her abdomen had lowered considerably. Emma helped pacify Bridget through each contraction, which was no easy feat as Bridget bitterly complained each was threatening to tear her asunder. By late afternoon, the labor was quickening and a servant was sent to fetch the doctor, who arrived with great haste. William took Clement out to the local tavern for a few drinks to pacify the frantic man.

By evening, Colin was imploring Bridget to push the babe forth into the world. Emma watched with awe and admiration as her fiancé calmly guided the squalling baby to the land of the living. She was filled with a new respect for what he did and loved him all the more. The baby was cleaned and placed in its mother's arms, who quickly forgot about the hours of pain and agony she had endured to bring it out.

Emma eagerly peered over. The baby boy was healthy and huge! She wondered how he could have come out of such a small woman. Bridget cooed over her new son and quickly offered him her breast to suckle. She was a natural and fit into the role of motherhood like a glove.

"What are you going to name him?" Emma asked as she sat on the edge of the bed, running a finger over the damp, fine blonde hair of the boy. The trio were alone, Rose and Colin having gone downstairs to tidy up and get a much-needed cup of coffee.

Bridget stared down in adoration at the mewling infant. "I want him to have a name of his own. I think I will call him Wade."

"That is a perfect name. We should write Will in the morning to tell him." She bestowed a kiss on mother and her new nephew, leaving them in peace.

After Wade's birth, all correspondence ceased from Will. Many of the other families in the area experienced the same silence from their loved ones. It was soon determined the battles and marches must have picked up and therefore, the men had little time to write. William gave up hope of hearing from his youngest son and went about in a sort of morose haze. The women spent their time coddling little Wade, adoring every moment they had with the gorgeous boy. Rose showed him off at the Ladies' Society and all commented on how he was the spitting image of Will as a babe.

By the time Wade had been in the world two months, news filtered in of McClellan's march on Richmond, by order of President Lincoln. The reports were vague, but it seemed there had also been sea battles along the peninsula. Union troops continued to advance on the Confederate forces and, for a short time, things seemed hopeful. However, July brought a crushing blow to the Union when McClellan was forced to retreat.

The summer heat smothered the household in stark contrast to the bitter winter. The ladies took to bringing Wade out on the porch in the evenings to try and get some fresh air. A positive to the warmer weather were the picnics and long walks after church on Sunday. However, there was a day quickly approaching Emma dreaded. There had been talk amongst the remaining men of their small corner of the world. It appeared doctors were in high demand to man the field hospitals, as well as the battlefield. Colin broke the news to his fiancée one evening as they walked through the park.

"I feel the time has come, Emma. It's my duty as a citizen and a doctor to help those in need." They had paused to sit on a bench.

Emma was struggling to maintain her composure. They had not heard from Will in a number of months and tensions were becoming high. Emma's father all but gave Harrison up for dead. Bridget went from fearing the worst to believing he would come in the door any moment. Rose's nerves were on tenterhooks as she was left caring for Bridget and Wade. Emma helped the best she could, but found herself frazzled as well when reports of wounded and missing started arriving on a daily basis.

"You cannot leave me, Colin! Please!" The normally strong woman collapsed into his arms, her body wracked with sobs.

Colin's heart was torn between wanting to stay and his duty to go off and fight, as so many young men had done before him. "The truth is, Emma, I have stayed too long behind. I am beginning to be branded a coward. I must go. Not just to help, but for my honor."

"Damn your honor!" Emma flung herself away from him, "Damn you men and your wars!" She fled his side, ignorant to his pleas for her to return. Her heart was breaking not only at the loss of her first love, but the thought both her brothers could be dead on a battlefield somewhere, and poor Wade would never know his loving father.

Rose followed Emma upstairs as she burst through the front door in tears. She soothed her heartbroken daughter. "Hush. You know Colin would not be going if it was not absolutely necessary. He is a good man and does not deserve to be parted from you in such a manner."

Emma met her mother's gaze with a mix of shock and hurt. Never before had Rose gently scolded her daughter in such a manner. "Do you think I was too hard on him?"

Dabbing her daughter's tears with a lace trimmed handkerchief, Rose nodded, "Yes, and I warrant he is pacing our porch at this very moment trying to find the words to comfort you."

Colin slumped down onto the porch steps, his head in his hands. The internal struggle between his love for Emma and helping the wounded on the battlefield had kept him up late at night. He wondered if he should have been more sensitive to Emma's situation. Cursing softly to himself, Colin rose from the step and walked with purpose to the front door, raising his hand to knock. Before he could do so, the portal flew open and a red-eyed Emma stood before him.

Swallowing hard, Colin tried to begin, "Emma, I..."

She silenced his explanation with a kiss. "Forgive me. I was much too harsh on you, Colin. I know what you have to do, and I admire you for doing it. I suppose I was fearful I would lose you." She cast her gaze downward and a tear slipped over her cheek.

Colin's heart broke to pieces, and he gathered the woman into his arms. "I promise with every last breath in my being, I will come back to you safe and sound."

Her breath tickling his neck, Emma murmured, "Do not make promises you know you cannot keep, Colin. Please try to stay out of danger. I hope this damned war ends quickly and you can come back and marry me."

Taking a step back, Colin held her at arm's length, "You do not want to marry before I leave?"

Emma shook her head, "No. I do not want to have you for a moment and then live a lifetime without you."

5

Rochester, New York
Early August, 1862

My dearest Emma,

I will be honest, as you so often expect of me. This war is turning into a living hell. I have arrived at the end of a bloody week of battles. The Union is estimated to have lost nearly 16,000 men, with still many missing. With luck, I was placed with McClennan's regiment, the same as your brother. This is where my letter will turn even grimmer. William Mansfield, Second Lieutenant, is missing in action and presumed dead. Please trust me when I say I will do everything to verify this news within my power. I have also taken it upon myself to seek any information from the Confederate prisoners we had taken about your brother, Harrison. Alas, my efforts have been futile.

On a more personal matter, I miss you dearly. I dream of the day I can have you in my arms again. My admiration for your strength and endurance in times of difficulty keeps me persevering in the grips of so much devastation. I love you more than anything, and the thought of coming back

to you is ever present in my mind.
We march on.

All my affection,
Colin

Emma's voice shook as she read the opening paragraph of the letter to Rose and William in the parlor. It was the first personal message they had received from any of their loved ones in some time, and the news came as a shock to all three. Bridget was upstairs playing with Wade. They decided until verification came, they would spare her the information, fearing it would send her into a deeper depression.

"If I were a man, I would go after them!" Emma announced fervently.

Rose dabbed her eyes with her handkerchief. "And what good would it do us to lose three children? At least we have you here."

"But what good is it if I am left an only child, with no one to spend my life with? I feel so helpless!" She slumped onto the settee with a dramatic sigh.

William patted Emma on the shoulder, "Your mother is correct, my dear. It would do little good to lose all three of one's children. I wonder why we have not seen William's name on the casualty report. I do place my faith in Doctor McCafferty. He is in the correct position, thank God, to discover further information about our boys."

Emma quickly rose from her seat and gathered up her shawl. "I believe I will pay Mrs. Hastings a visit. She wished me to assist her in the last of the preparations for the hospital."

Hurrying along the sunbaked streets, Emma racked her brain for something she could do besides roll bandages. The hospital was due to open in October and would see many of the gravely injured men shipped back to Fort Schuyler, along with any prisoners of war. She wondered if Harrison would find himself back here in that capacity. The repercussions for his foolish actions were sure to be great. By the time Emma reached Mrs. Hastings' door, her mind was a flurry of ideas.

Millie escorted the flushed woman into the parlor where Mrs. Hastings waited. Upon seeing Emma's state, she quickly asked for refreshments and gestured to an armchair. "My dear! You look positively parched. What would possess you to come out at the warmest part of the day?"

"I am in desperate need of advice, ma'am." Emma graciously accepted the glass of lemonade placed into her hand by Millie, taking a long drink before continuing, "I feel so utterly helpless! We received a letter this morning from Colin, and Will is listed as missing in action, presumed dead. I know my brother, and he is not dead! I can feel it in my heart!"

"Calm yourself, Miss Mansfield. Where is your brother's unit?"

"I believe he and Colin are in the Army of the Potomac, at least it is what I assume since they are under General McClennan's command."

"You are an intuitive young lady, Emma. I am proud you are my protégée. Educated women will be prized in our society someday. Now, tell me, what would you like to do?"

Emma traced a droplet of condensation on the side of her glass. "You would not think it...becoming of a young lady."

Mrs. Hastings threw back her head in laughter, quickly explaining to Emma nothing shocked her in her old age, and she should know better, judging on her experiences with the elder woman. At her urging, Emma confessed her deepest desire was to go seek out her brothers and bring them back home safely. Leaning forward in her chair, Emma was informed her confession was not as outlandish as she believed.

At Emma's quizzical look, Mrs. Hastings went on to explain about a woman who had dressed up and enlisted in the Confederate Army under the name of John Williams. Although, her time in the army was short-lived, she managed to evade detection until her husband was injured. At that time, she revealed her secret, and was discharged along with her spouse.

"So you see, my dear, where there is a will, there is a way." Mrs. Hastings smiled conspiratorially, and took a sip of her cool drink.

A picture of pure shock and curiosity, Emma placed her empty glass down, "Surely, you are not suggesting I dress as a man and enlist in the Union Army!"

"That is precisely what I am suggesting."

"What about training? And my face...hair? I hardly look like a man."

Mrs. Hastings tapped her fingers on the brocade of the chair, "There would have to be some sacrifices made on your part. Hair grows back again. As for military tactics, all those enlisted go through a training camp. Many young men from our city have never fired rifles or cannons before. You are strong from working in your father's shop during his absence, so I have no doubt that you will pass your training course with flying colors.

"I do recommend you push for artillery training. Those farthest away from the battlefield are in less danger. I have several books on the subject. We could easily pass you as a young apprentice, my long-lost nephew." Standing, she went to a bookshelf and removed several tomes on the topic, passing them to Emma, "I believe you are an avid reader, yes?"

Emma mindlessly nodded, "Why do you have these?"

Waving her hand in the air, Mrs. Hastings laughed. "What, a woman is not allowed to have such unladylike interests? Mr. Hastings spoke of artillery constantly. The science and the mechanics of such military instruments have long been a fascination of mine and I keep myself up-to-date on the newest advancements. Go and learn all you can. Return to me in two weeks' time. If you have not changed your mind, I will instruct you on how to proceed."

Prince William County, Virginia
August 30, 1862

Lieutenant Will Mansfield brushed the mud from his face, remaining low in the brush, hunching his shoulders. He could hear voices around him, but being unsure of their military origins, chose to remain silent until they drew near. He had a gash in his upper left arm, but was otherwise unhurt. Will recalled the last battle he fought as he lay there, wondering if he would face capture or death. He remembered being at Malvern Hill, as the fighting raged, mainly among the artillery forces. General Robert E. Lee of the Confederacy had put up a fight, but underestimated the power of the Union forces. In the end, Lee withdrew and the Union Army ended up encamped near Berkeley Plantation, the birthplace of William Henry Harrison, ninth president of the United States.

By the end of the seven days of fighting, both sides had taken heavy losses and the Peninsula Campaign came to an end. Will was listed under the some six thousand men missing or captured, although he did not know it at the time. Shoddy counting on the part of the military made him go unnoticed in the massive trudge across Virginia. As he lay in the damp earth, surrounded by bodies of his fellow soldiers, Will longed for Bridget's soft arms and warm caresses. Surely she would have had their child by now, and he longed to know if it was a boy or a girl, but letters were scarce.

By some miracle, he had survived, only to march into another battle. Because General McClellan had been relieved of duty by President Lincoln, they were now under the leading command of Major General John Pope. The Second Battle of Manassas was a loss for the Union Army, much like the first. There were casualties, again, on both sides and Will prayed there would be an opportunity for the Union forces to gather their wounded, and bury the dead.

"Over here! Check these men!" A familiar voice broke through Will's daydreams. He chanced a glimpse and scanned the surroundings. A tall man in emerald green was directing some infantrymen to examine the bodies strewn about. Squinting, Will seemed to recognize the medical corps officer, but could not place him. Stumbling to his feet, he waved an arm.

The officer strode over and took a small pause, "William Mansfield? Lieutenant William Mansfield?" The shock was evident in his voice.

Will coughed and held a hand over his bleeding wound. "Yes, sir." He identified the man to be a captain.

Smiling widely, the captain ushered him back to the temporary hospital set up for triage, "I know someone will be very relieved you are alive."

While stitching up the injury, Will became quickly acquainted with the medical officer. Captain Colin McCafferty was bemused by the fact he had stumbled on his future brother-in-law in such an unlikely manner.

"They thought I was missing in action? I am not surprised. There were so many casualties, some of the boys were blown to bits." Will shuddered at the memory. His best friends seemed to explode right before his eyes on the second day of fighting. Will took it upon himself to write their mother a letter, explaining their deaths and applauding their bravery. It was still tucked safely in his jacket.

"You are very lucky we found you. I will have to write a letter to your sister and tell her the happy news." Colin cleared his throat and busied himself bandaging the wound.

Will quirked a brow, "You must be something to have won Emma's heart. I have never known her to take to any man, although many tried. If you have the ability to post letters, I would like to take advantage of your connections, if

I may?"

Unable to keep the grin from spreading on his face, Captain McCafferty finished attending to Lieutenant Mansfield. "Of course. We should get the rest of the men back to safer ground. I hate to say it, but many will not survive the trip."

"Can I help in any way? This wound is relatively superficial. In fact, I feel ashamed you've wasted your time on me."

Chuckling lightly, Colin wiped his hands, "Emma would have my head if I did not."

With the help of the young lieutenant, wounded men were loaded into wagons and withdrawn to safety. Before returning to his commanding officer and correcting the error of his status, Will penned quick missives to Bridget and his parents. He was comforted by the thought they would rejoice at the revelation he was alive and in the company of the captain. Restored to his status, Will was transferred back under the command of McClellan, marching up to Maryland.

Rochester, New York
Early September, 1862

Emma returned to the Hastings' residence two weeks after her last visit, as promised. Mrs. Hastings guided her upstairs to a guest room. On the bed was a perfectly tailored artillery uniform, trimmed in red.

"I took the liberty of having this made for you. We need to come up with a name." Tapping a finger to her lips in thought, Mrs. Hastings watched Emma run her hand over the brass buttons.

"Just like Will's..." Tears welled at the corners of her eyes.

Emma was shocked by the slap she received. "None of

this! You must not cry. Harden your heart, as you will see things that would shock the delicate sensibilities of other ladies."

Recovering from her bout of weakness, Emma raised her chin with an air of defiance, "Will used to call me 'Em' when we were younger. Perhaps some variation, so I do not get confused."

"Good thinking, my dear. Perhaps we could call you...Emmett? Ah, yes, that would be perfect. Emmett Hastings...no, Hawkins. That is close enough. Can you remember the name?" Mrs. Hastings seemed to be living vicariously through Emma, and if she were younger, Emma supposed it would be she who was going off to battle.

Emma repeated the name slowly and secured it in her memory. Mrs. Hastings conveyed her to a dressing table in the room with a pair of scissors on the vanity. Emma elicited a small gasp, not expecting the transition to take place so soon.

"I cannot write a letter to explain to my parents?"

Shaking her head, Mrs. Hastings began to pluck pins from Emma's mane of hair as she spoke, "No, my dear. You must not tell anyone where you have gone, or who you are. I will speak to your parents and tell them you are accompanying me on a short journey. When I return, I will break the news."

Emma closed her eyes and prayed. The snip of the shears made her want to sob, as ringlets fell around her. When she finally opened her emerald green eyes, shimmering with unshed tears, Emma was met with an unfamiliar face. Her hair had been shorn to a length befitting a young man. Mrs. Hastings had done an admirable job wielding the scissors.

"There. One more thing before we take you to the enlistment office. Clothing off, my dear."

Emma gasped, having never been seen naked by another person, save her mother. "I..."

"We have to bind your breasts, Emma. They are a dead

giveaway to your female state." The statement was made matter-of-factly, with no pretense. Emma allowed the older woman to help her disrobe and perform the needed task. When she peered in the mirror again, Emma was as flat-chested as any man. Repeating the task several times, Emma learned to perform the necessary function herself.

For the next hour, Mrs. Hastings schooled her in how to walk like a man, and lower her voice appropriately. She gave her a pair of trousers, boots, and a collared shirt. Emma found the freedom of movement liberating, if not a bit strange. Together, they left the house. To the untrained eye, they appeared to be no more than an elderly woman and a young male family member out for a stroll in the afternoon sun.

Emma repeated slowly in her head. "I am Emmett Hawkins."

The sun shone bright in the sky, punctuating the crisp, autumn air. Emma did her best to gather her thoughts. She was putting her life at risk to run a fool's errand. What would Colin think? Would he still want to marry her? No, this was something she had to do, or nothing would save her from the criticism of her own mind. As they approached the small office which served as the enlistment quarters for the Union Army, Emma hesitated, leaning over to Mrs. Hastings, "What if I forget something?"

"You are an apprentice, my dear. It is not expected for you to be an expert in artillery. Show them you are worthy of the regiment." With those reassuring words, she escorted Emma into the room. There was a man dressed in uniform sitting behind a desk. He eyed the pair suspiciously. Mrs. Hastings took the lead.

"Good afternoon, sir. My recently arrived nephew has a desire to serve in the Union Army." Her tone was authoritative, and the man straightened, scrutinizing the youth carefully.

"Name?"

"Emmett Hawkins, sir." Emma's voice cracked, and she cleared her throat.

"Age?"

"Eighteen this past spring, sir."

The uniformed officer stood. Emma immediately recognized his rank as a Captain by the double gold bars on his epaulettes. He was also a West Point graduate, she surmised, based on the tailoring of his uniform jacket.

"Eighteen you say? You do not look much older than sixteen."

Mrs. Hastings withdrew a packet of papers from her drawstring bag. Emma had to prevent her mouth from gaping open. She had thought of everything to protect Emma's identity. "As you can see, Captain, my nephew is of age. He would also be of use."

"Has he no tongue? Boy, what can you do?"

Emma swallowed hard, lowering her voice, "My father, sir, was a gunsmith. I am well versed with artillery, sir."

"Being the son of a gunsmith tells me nothing. Did you apprentice your father, Hawkins?"

Emma quickly nodded, "Yes, sir."

"What cannons are we using on the Eastern front?"

Her mind raced, trying to recall the facts that had been so hastily jammed-packed into her mind. "The Napoleon, sir, and variations thereof. It's easily maneuverable and has a range of approximately 1200 yards, although the distance can change based on elevation."

The Captain was clearly impressed and he returned to his desk. "Clever lad. We can make use of you. Are you strong?"

"Of mind, sir. I am not afraid of hard work."

"Sign here. You depart as soon as we can get a wagon. McClennan's men can use you."

Emma almost began to cry. She had been assigned where Will was, and her beloved Colin. What luck! She composed herself, and squared her shoulders. "Thank you, sir."

After filling out the applicable paperwork, they departed the office. Neither was aware of an officer standing nearby, back to the wall, hat brim low over his shaggy hair. He stubbed out his cigar on the sole of his boot and moved back into the office, a scowl on his face.

Emma returned to Mrs. Hastings' residence. She was mentally exhausted from the experience and asked to rest in one of the upstairs rooms. A telegram arrived while she was asleep. Emmett Hawkins would join the ranks of the Army of the Potomac in the artillery corps. From that moment forward, Emma Mansfield ceased to exist.

Battle of Antietam
Sharpsburg, Maryland
September 17th, 1862

My sweet Emma,

I will send this letter as soon as I am able. We are inundated with wounded and dying men. I had hoped to spare you this portion of my service, but I know you would not forgive me if I were not truthful. Please spare Mrs. Mansfield and your mother the grisly details of which I am about to impart. Men lay in their own blood on the battlefield. The fighting raged all day. We estimate 12,000 men are wounded, dead, or missing. You will be pleased to know your dear brother is not among those dead or wounded. He fought admirably and sends his regards to you all.

General Lee has retreated across the Potomac and we have considered this battle a victory. I am still unsure as to how so many young men perishing in the course of a fruitless battle can be considered victory. How I long to be in your arms and feel your soft skin against my hands.

All my love,
Colin

The Battle of Antietam was the first major battle of the

Civil War to take place on Union soil. In total, nearly 23,000 men lost their lives. There was never a proclaimed victor, but the Union took it as a victory for their side, and it was never disputed. General McClellan of the Union Army had pursued General Robert E. Lee of the Confederacy into the state of Maryland. The strategic victory by the Union Army lead to the president announcing the pending Emancipation Proclamation, which would be finalized in the coming year. Em, as he came to be known by his compatriots, was sitting in training camp when the news came through.

It had been an exhausting day of marching and drills. Emmett kept up with his fellow recruits, working as hard as any of them. Some of the men commented on the boy's lithe figure and quick reflexes, admiring his speed and ingenuity. Others were jealous of the favor the boy rapidly gained with his knowledge of artillery. After Antietam, there was little time to lose. Men were needed to replace those who perished in battle. The army was marching back towards Virginia, and this was where the new recruits would meet them.

Em kept to himself most of the time, choosing to maintain a distance from the rest of the men, scribbling in a leather-bound journal. He was careful to keep the things he recorded as neutral as possible, not wanting to reveal the secret carried deep within his breast. There were times Em forgot he was a woman beneath the uniform. It was probably for the best he maintained his disguise to the fullest.

Letters to his family were impossible, except the occasional one to his aunt, letting her know he was still alive and well. The last one was sent as they left training camp for the march south.

Dearest Aunt,

We have completed our basic training and are marching to meet the army. I cannot reveal more for fear this letter will be intercepted. Please know I am doing well and excelling, much to the joy of my superiors. I will find him, Aunt. Please give my regards to the Mansfields, especially to Baby W.

Until next time,
Em

Mrs. Hastings tucked each letter away. Her plan was to reveal Emma's location when she knew the girl was safely out of reach. Rose had come to her home frantic about the disappearance of her only daughter. With gentle words, Mrs. Hastings kept Emma's secret, but reassured her mother she was safe, and volunteering in a hospital for the wounded. Knowing her father would forbid any more of his children from entering into the clutches of the war, Emma came to Mrs. Hastings for help in the matter. They found her a post, and Emma departed. Rose was clearly heartbroken, but understood. William raged for several days, soon coming around to the departure as well. Emma's cover was now secure.

Antietam, Maryland
October, 1862

Will, finally, received a letter after many months of little communication from his family. It was penned in his mother's hand and dated before what he could only assume was the birth of his child. The delay in family correspondence from home caused many of the men to grow restless. Will took out his tintype of Bridget and traced his finger over her face. The memories of their last night together surfaced as if it were yesterday.

Bridget had been so shy the blood rose in her cheeks, but Will soon coaxed her into their bed with tender kisses and caresses. It was in that passion-filled night they must have conceived their child. It nearly destroyed him to think he would never see his babe, or feel his wife's sweet breath on his neck as she slept. Tucking the portrait back into his breast pocket, he let out a sigh. The night was quiet, the song of crickets echoing through the air. He barely noticed when Colin joined him, wiping the sweat from his brow.

"We've managed to ship the worse ones off to a hospital up North. Who knows if they will even survive the journey?"

Will gave him a sympathetic pat on the shoulder, "You did what you could."

Colin shook his head, "Some of them...their insides were hanging out, Will. You patch them up the best you can and make them comfortable. There was nothing I could do for some of them. We are lucky we can at least give them some morphine to dull the pain, but supplies are running short. How can I uphold my oath to heal the sick and injured when so many are dying in my care?"

"War is hell, Colin. We do the best we can to fight for what we believe is right."

"How do you keep going? How do you keep killing men?"

Will looked down at his dusty, mud-caked boots. "I do not know. Maybe because each man I kill brings me one step closer to home and Bridget."

"Will...I am sorry I did not tell you sooner. Bridget had her child before I left. A boy. His name is Wade." Colin had kept the news a secret for reasons he did not even begin to understand.

Will glanced over, "You kept this from me?" He was too fatigued to argue reasoning with the doctor.

"I am sorry. I had hoped we would receive more letters, and you could see it in Mrs. Mansfield's own hand." Colin rubbed his brow, "It was foolish."

Amidst the horrors of war, Will thought better than to start another battle with the man who would be his brother-in-law. "I accept your apology." Will glanced up at the men gathered around his small fire. They tended to stay grouped based on regiment, mostly for companionship.

Will vaguely took notice of a slim boy, sitting alone, by the artillery soldiers. His shoulders were hunched as he scribbled in a notebook. Will could make out the streak of gunpowder smoke across his cheeks. He removed his hat and ran a hand through his thinly-cropped, auburn hair, turning his face to the sky for a moment to catch a breath of fresh air. The mannerisms appeared quite familiar to Will, but he could not place his finger on where he had seen them before.

"Col, that boy there..." Will gestured, leaving the sentence unfinished.

Colin followed the movement of Will's hand to observe the younger lad. "One of the new recruits. They arrived just before the battle. Hard workers from our hometown, I think."

Will shook his head, "I cannot remember anyone of that description from home."

Colin shrugged, "Maybe he's kin to someone nearby? You could just ask him."

"That is a good idea. Perhaps he has news of Bridget?" Will pushed himself to his feet and sauntered over, his shadow casting a dark specter on the dirt. The boy gazed upward and paled considerably, before clearing his throat.

Will began to speak without making eye contact, "So, Private, are you well?"

The youth shoved his hat firmly on his head and lowered the brim, "Yes, Sir, as well as one can be in the circumstances."

"Where do you come from?"

"New York, sir, I have an aunt there."

Will's heart leapt, "What is her name?" It was a shot in the dark. New York was a big state.

"Hastings, sir. Elizabeth Hastings."

Will grabbed the boy with a little more force than necessary, and hauled him to his feet. His kepi tumbled from his head, and Will was met with a pair of scared, dull green eyes. Finally focusing on the lad for the first time, Will felt his breath hitch. "Em..."

The boy cut him off, "Emmett Hawkins, sir. I came to live with my aunt after my parents died." His eyes narrowed threateningly as he squared his shoulders.

"You...Tonight. Here. Once your regiment goes to sleep. That's an order." Spinning on his heel, Will returned to Colin, who gave him a quizzical glance.

Will clenched his teeth. "It's Emma."

Emma sat trembling after her encounter with Will. He would send her home, without a doubt. She could not let it happen! Knowing Will was safe had spurred her on to an even greater mission: to find out if Harrison was alive. She peered over at the pair of men, immediately recognizing the stance of the captain. Her heart sank further. If Colin knew she was here, he would have to reveal her identity and discharge her.

After a quick mental debate with herself, Emma made the decision to attempt to get herself transferred. She had already proved herself worthy in the face of battle. Perhaps there was a chance to escape her older brother's meddling after all. Silently gathering her things, she hightailed it to the closest command tent, and made her plea.

When Will arrived to the appointed meeting spot that evening, Colin close on his heels, he was furious to see that Emma was not there waiting for them. He paced restlessly beneath the tree, muttering about how foolish her actions were. Colin stared out into the black night, punctuated by flickering campfires.

"Maybe something happened?" Although he admired her fortitude, Colin was petrified at the thought of Emma getting injured, and her gender revealed to unfamiliar faces.

Will crossed his arms, "I know exactly what happened." He turned on his heel, making a beeline for the command tent. Lifting the flap, he observed the officers partaking in cigars and brandy.

"What can we do for you two gentlemen?" There was a hint of irritation in the tone of the man who spoke, the two outsiders having disturbed their futile attempt at civility.

"Apologies, sir, but I am seeking information about one of the men in the artillery unit. A young private by the name of Emmett Hawkins, sir."

One member of the party straightened in his chair, "Has the boy done something, Lieutenant?"

Will straightened his back, "No, sir, not that I know of."

"Well, don't worry about the boy. He requested a transfer."

"A transfer?" Colin and Will had spoken at the same time, without even realizing it.

The collected officers laughed and one spoke, "I didn't know one private could cause so much of a stir. We did not have anywhere new to send him, so we assigned him to a supply unit. They marched out an hour ago. They should be back in a few weeks. Now, if there aren't any more issues...?"

Both men saluted, and withdrew from the tent. Colin faced Will, "He's not weak, Will. He will be fine." His change of pronoun was as much for his peace of mind as Will's.

"I hope you're right."

"Get some sleep. I have patients to check over before we ship the rest of them home, lucky devils." Colin clapped him on the shoulder, and strode off to the makeshift hospital tent.

Will thought of heading back to his tent to rest, but he could not settle his mind. Writing home would only worry their mother and father. He silently made a pact to drag Emma to the first officer's tent he could get to when she got back and get her sent home.

Back in the hospital tent, Colin made his rounds. Many of the men needed surgery and treatment he could not offer in the conditions. Taking a seat behind the rickety desk, Colin completed the necessary paperwork for the transfers to the larger hospital in Annapolis. He heard several barns had been converted for hospital usage. Colin could not begin to imagine the hygienic conditions, but he supposed needs must in the drastic situation.

Pulling out his leather-bound journal, Colin leaned back in the chair and penned a short missive to Emma:

Since writing to you would be a fruitless effort, I will share my thoughts through this journal, in hopes I will be able to show them to you after this war ends. I know you are here, and I know why. While I am fearful for your safety, I would be destroying everything I love about you by preventing you from doing this task. Please keep yourself alert.

His pen hovered above the page, unsure how to continue. The feeling of helplessness overwhelmed him. Angrily, he slammed the journal shut and folded his hands together, praying she was unharmed.

Near Cumberland, Maryland
November 1862

Emma trudged along with the supply unit, the straps of her leather backpack digging into her neck. The pain was only intensified by the Springfield rifle bouncing on her right shoulder with each step. Mud caked her shoes. The rattle of the wagon behind her became a dull drone in her ears. To add insult to injury, a cold drizzle began to fall, soaking the wool of their uniforms. Trying to remain alert became a chore within itself.

When the unit finally rested to set up camp, the rain was coming down in sheets. Emma attempted to dry her uniform by the fire. The men sat huddled around the warmth, steam flooding off the drenched wool. She wrinkled her nose, reminded of the smell of their family dog having come into the kitchen seeking comfort from a storm. It was funny the things she had begun to recall in these quiet moments.

Emma sought refuge in her small tent. The other men quickly got used to the youth's need for privacy, and refrained from the quick jibes and teasing. Em had proven himself in the Battle of Antietam, braving direct fire to retrieve more powder for their cannons. The "powder monkey," as the adolescent soldiers were often called, was crucial to the success of the artillery campaigns.

Safe within the confines of her tent, Emma unwound the dirty, sweat-soaked length of cloth used to bind her breasts and sighed with relief. She only allowed herself a momentary reprieve from the bonds, lest someone from the unit come across her. With how some of them spoke, Emma shuddered to think what they would do upon her discovery. These men were not used to being without a woman for so long, and the camp followers were often riddled with disease.

Using some of her precious water, Emma cleansed herself and redressed, making sure to tighten the fabric. Over the bindings, she lowered her grey linen shirt, tucking it into the sky-blue trousers and fastening the tin buttons. Shrugging into the slightly large overcoat, Emma shuddered at the feel of the damp wool, but was grateful for the added coverage. She replaced her brogans with a pair of boots, knowing they would hurt her feet, but provide added protection from the elements.

Placing down her bedroll, Emma used her backpack as a pillow. She fell into a restless sleep, haunted by visions of men blown to bits by cannon fire. When the orders were given the following morning to pack up and march out, Emma was just as exhausted as she had been the previous night. Falling into line with the rest of the unit, the weary travelers made their way into Cumberland.

Cumberland, Maryland was established as a Union stronghold early in the war. Union troops were garrisoned there to protect the B&O Railroad line from Confederate raids. The strategic location of Cumberland provided protection to Washington D.C. as well as other areas of Virginia. It was a vital lifeline to the Union war efforts. Having recently fended off another attack, the men were on guard.

Emma stood guard at the wagon, while several of the men began to fill it with food, weapons, and other supplies. It was a risky run, but needed if the men were going to withstand another battle with Confederate forces. Out of the corner of her eye, she saw several Union soldiers rounding up some prisoners of war, probably from the last raid. Biting the inside of her cheek, Emma quickly recognized one of them to be her brother, Harrison. Straining to hear the conversation above the thud of crates into the wagon, Emma took a small step closer.

"Lazy good-for-nothing Rebs! What do you know? Attacking your own country!" One of the Union soldiers lashed out, and hit a captive in the belly with his rifle butt. The man groaned and hunched forward. Harrison quickly moved to support the crumpling figure.

"What's the matter? Can't hold your own?" The soldiers began to chuckle. Emma saw red and abandoned her post, marching over.

"Hey! Captured men have rights! I should report you to your superior!" She raised her chin defiantly.

"Aww, look! It's a little powder monkey!" The soldier squared up to her, "Lost?"

"Nope. On a supply run. From the front. More than what you've been doing!"

Raising his fist, the confrontation was stopped abruptly by a passing officer. After getting the story from all parties, the abusive Union soldier was duly reprimanded. His glare at Emma told her he would not soon forget their interaction. As the prisoners were led away, Harrison squinted at Emma, but recognition did not pass over his face. She returned to her ranks, and they began the long march back to the front lines.

Emma marched in silence, sending up a quiet prayer of thanks. Her youngest brother was alive and captured. She hoped he would be merely held until the end of the war, and then returned home to the loving arms of his family. Father would certainly forgive his impulsive nature, and they could get back to their lives.

"Pretty brave there, Hawkins. None of us would have had

the guts to stand up to that blowhard." Emma recognized the young private from her unit. Billy Rawlings was from a poorer part of New York. His upbringing was a contrast to Emma's, but he worked just as hard. In the army, there were no social classes, only ranks.

Emma shrugged, "I suppose, I just think people shouldn't be treated like that. We're all human beings."

Billy grinned, "Suppose you're right, Hawkins. That's some pretty fancy philosophy there."

Fixing her gaze ahead, Emma smiled, "My ma, she was a smart lady. Told me that we should respect others, no matter what they look like."

"Guess so. She one of them abolitionist people?"

Emma nodded, "Yes. She died of a fever before I went to live with my aunt."

"Sorry to hear that. Hey, maybe this here Emancipation thing will be good? Darkies can come fight for us!" Billy clapped her hard on the back, and Emma remained silent. He continued on, "Hey, I heard that McClellan's been dismissed. We have a new general."

Emma inclined her head, vaguely interested in the political motivations behind a change in command, "Rawlings, what do you think'll happen to those men from the town?"

"The Rebs? Dunno. Probably get traded back, I bet."

"Traded back?" Emma's heart skipped a beat.

Billy gave her a look of concern, "You alright? You've gone pretty pale, Hawkins."

"Yeah, yeah. Just tired."

"It has been a long day. We'll be back soon."

The realization dawned on Emma. She would have to face Will once they returned. Hopefully, everyone would be more concerned with the advance, so he would not have time to confront her. As they rolled into the main encampment, the air was electrified. They were greeted with the news of Burnside taking over the Army of the Potomac. An advance on the Confederate capital of Richmond was planned, and the army would march out as soon as humanly possible. The men were buzzing with excitement at the approaching engagement.

Emma slipped away from the crowds, her desire to be alone pressing in on her. She had a headache and wanted nothing more than to escape the raucous voices. Shielding herself with a tree, Emma slumped to the ground. *How did I think I could do this? Harrison and Will are alive, but for how much longer?* She buried her face in her hands, as her body shuddered, tormented by silent weeping.

Colin watched the revelry over the encroaching battle with little emotion. The men had been camped in Warrington, Virginia, awaiting orders to advance. Colin knew he had to steel himself against the influx of wounded and dying men sure to be in his immediate future. Circling the camp, Colin could understand why the men were excited to make a crucial strike at the enemy. Spotting a backpack by a tree, he approached, and discovered a crumpled youth sitting at the opposite side.

"Soldier?" Colin knelt by the boy, his voice soothing.

Visibly stiffening, the boy coughed and sniffed loudly, saying nothing.

"It's a lot to take, I know. You miss your folks?"

Shaking, the boy shook his head, keeping his face covered by the kepi. Colin touched his shoulder, "It'll be okay, son. We will all be home soon." He caught glimpse of an auburn tendril of hair under the cap, and something stirred in his stomach. Positioning himself in front of the youth, he carefully removed the hat and lifted his chin.

Emma's reddened eyes met his, her lips trembling. *Oh, Colin. I'm so sorry.* The words did not come.

Colin replaced the cap, "Stand up." His voice was firm, but held no trace of anger. Supporting her under the elbow,

Colin retrieved the pack. Guiding Emma to the hospital tent, he entered, reporting the soldier had exhaustion and dehydration. No one seemed to question his orders and a space was cleared at the end of the large tent with a screen. The vestibule was almost empty, save a young man sleeping on a cot with a gash on his brow.

Colin lowered Emma's body to the cot and moved to open the coat. She fought him, but he hushed her, placing a kiss on her feverish brow. Glad to be shielded by the barrier, Colin inspected Emma closely, determining she needed a good sleep in a warm bed. Thankfully, they would not be departing for a day or so. Slipping off her boots, he tucked a blanket around her and temporarily withdrew.

Colin abruptly informed the private assigned to the medical unit that he would take the nightshift. The private offered no objection, glad for the reprieve to socialize with the other men and dream of glory in battle. Retrieving a wooden chair, Colin returned to Emma's bedside where she slept fitfully. In his hand, he carried his notebook, opening it up to a blank page to write.

My sweet Emma,

Here you are, laying before me. Your complexion is ashen, so unlike the woman I took to the social nearly a year ago. Has it been that long since I laughed? I want to gather your form into my arms and carry you away from all this. Would you grow to forgive me if I took you away? I should find Will and tell him you are back. He would most certainly send you away. The one thing I want to do is protect you, but no matter how I look at it, I would be driving you away. I will do what I can to shield you.

The pen fell to the page as Emma stirred, her eyes fluttering open and focusing on his face. She smiled at him dreamily and Colin lost all his self-control. He sat on the cot and gathered her into his arms, whispering huskily, "My sweet Emma."

Emma grew startled and frantically looked around, like a frightened animal. Colin quickly reassured her they were alone and rubbed her back until she relaxed in his embrace. "Emma, what possessed you to come out here?"

"I had to find Will and Harrison." She murmured softly against his neck.

Pressing his lips to her temple, Colin refrained from telling her he was more than capable of the task. He ran his fingers through her shorn hair, tilting her head up and covering her mouth with his. She gasped at the intimate gesture and pulled back slightly.

"Someone might come in."

Colin slipped the jacket from her shoulders, "No, I've relieved the private of duty, and the rest of them are having one last hurrah before the battle march."

That was all the reassurance Emma needed. Her fingers fumbled with the brass buttons of his overcoat, a sudden urge to feel someone alive and warm overwhelming her being. Colin pulled her shirt from the waistband of her trousers, his roving fingertips encountering the fabric that concealed her rounded breasts. Her skin was still silken to his touch and he lifted the shirt over her head.

"Colin..." Her voice was sweet and pleading as he devoured her lips with kisses, nibbling on them and tangling his tongue with hers. Twirling the fabric from her body, Colin brought his hands around her breasts, tweaking the nipples gently before lowering his mouth to taste her sweet flesh.

Emma arched her back and moaned as his tongue drew wicked circles around the pliant peaks. She divested him of his shirt and placed her palms on his warm chest, drawing him down on top of her on the small cot. Somehow in the flurry of enthusiastic need, they removed the rest of their clothing and Colin's manhood pressed into her tender belly.

Studying her with love-filled eyes, Colin waited for her consent before initiating an act reserved for married couples. Emma's thighs were resting against his hips. Her nails raked down his back as she arched up. He took the silent signals and slowly slid inside her. Her wet sheath was tight and hot. Placing a hand over her mouth to stifle her cries, Colin thrust hard, taking Emma's virginity.

A single tear slipped down her cheek, but soon, all pain was forgotten as he drove her higher and higher, until they both reached the pinnacle of ecstasy. Colin collapsed gently on top of her small form with a sigh of contentment and hurried declarations of love. Emma was floating on air and not ashamed of her actions. Life had to be lived in the moment. If either of them perished in the upcoming conflict, they would always have this night of pure love.

Advance on Fredericksburg, Virginia
Late November, 1862

Major General Burnside had the Army of the Potomac moving with rapid speed towards the capital of the Confederacy. They broke camp early and began the advance towards Fredericksburg. It was a nearly forty-mile march and there was little time to stop. Burnside had approved the plan with Lincoln, who urged Burnside to make his move as quickly as possible. Lincoln was disappointed with the slow advance of his troops under McClellan, and hoped Burnside would provide a fresher view on the military tactics of the Union Army.

The units moved swiftly into Fredericksburg, taking the Confederate Army by surprise. General Robert E. Lee did not expect such a rapid advance. He had separated his military forces, leaving Fredericksburg woefully vulnerable to attack. However, there was an obstacle Burnside had not anticipated. The Union forces needed to traverse the Rappahannock River unopposed, but weather was making it nearly impossible. Bridges had been destroyed very early on in the war. By the time preparations had been made, Lee had recalled troops to guard the banks.

It was late in the evening and Emma sat near the fire with a few of her fellow soldiers. There was murmured discussion of Burnside's plans on how to get across the Rappahannock.

"He's crazy," Billy muttered, "There's no way we can get across without becoming cannon fodder for the Rebs."

"Burnside is a smart man. Lincoln wouldn't have put him in charge if he thought he was stupid." Another powder monkey, Richard Bates, piped up. His endless optimism and blind faith in their commanding officers sometimes irritated the other soldiers.

"That's what they said about McClellan, Rich." Billy threw a stick onto the fire and watched the flames lick at the curling bark.

Emma gazed up at the black sky, letting out a wisp of clouded breath, "Do you think we will be home for Christmas?"

Billy stared at her, shocked to hear the first words Emma had spoken since they departed towards Fredericksburg, "I don't think so, Em. This war is gonna last longer than they thought, I reckon."

"Do you miss your family?" Emma felt a small pang in her chest as Wade's chubby-cheeked smile came into her mind.

Pulling out his knife, Billy began to whittle another piece of wood as if he needed something to do with his hands to ward off the nerves building inside him. "I reckon I do a bit. My ma, she'll be worried. My dad is probably off getting drunk somewhere. I wanted to make a name for my family, ya know? Heck, I might die tomorrow..."

Emma touched his arm, "You won't die, Billy. We'll make it back."

Billy stared at her hand for a moment, "You know, Em, you're a strange sort of soldier."

Withdrawing her hand, Emma cleared her throat, eliciting a deep sort of cough, "How so?"

"You care. Many men, they don't care about what happens to us." Billy fished around in his pocket, "Can you write, Em?"

Emma nodded and Billy continued, "Can you write some stuff for me? I did okay in school, but I wasn't one for fancy words."

Accepting the pen and paper from Billy, Emma listened to him dictate a letter to his mother. It was the type of letter many of the men carried pinned into their jackets. She had to bite the inside of her cheek to keep from tearing up. Emma could not risk writing one herself, for fear it would fall into the wrong hands.

When they finished, Emma passed the letter to Billy for his signature. He tucked it away in his coat, "Em, if something happens, send it to my ma, okay?"

"Nothing will happen to us, Billy." Although the words passed her lips, Emma wasn't sure she believed them anymore.

They sat huddled around the warmth of the flames until word began to slowly trickle through the camp about Burnside's plans to cross the river. Emma had not seen Colin or Will since they departed the camp in Warrington. The thought of her passionate tussle with Colin in the hospital tent still sent shivers down her body. Emma clung to those whispered endearments and promises of everlasting love.

Billy leaned over to Emma, interrupting her train of thought, "We'll be sitting ducks if the Rebs get here before we cross."

Studying him quizzically, Emma had not heard the news of the advance, "What do you mean?"

"Burnside wants us to cross the river, but who knows when he will get to supplies?"

Emma squinted out at the murky water lapping the shoreline. A foreboding feeling crept into her heart.

By the time the supplies to cross the river reached the Union troops, the Army of North Virginia occupied the bank opposite their camp. It would take a few more tense weeks before any action came. Burnside was at odds with his lieutenants. Finally, a plan was made to build three crossings and hope the men made it across. Billy came up to Emma as she was packing away her things. He had a grim look on his face.

"I've been assigned to help build the bridges. We are starting early tomorrow." Holding out his hand, Billy continued, "If I get killed, don't forget to send my letter. In fact, take it now. Please, Em."

The folded paper was wrinkled from being in his pocket. Emma took it with a nod and a small smile. "Good luck, Billy."

Billy smiled back. "You too, Em."

No one slept much the night prior to the river crossing. In the pre-dawn hours, the Union engineers began laying out the supplies for the pontoons. After completing two of the bridges, they moved upriver. Shots rang out and the men scrambled for their rifles. Burnside ordered his artillery chief, Brigadier General Henry Hunt, to gather his men and take position above the city. If they couldn't charge the Confederate forces, they would blast the town into surrender.

Around noon, Emma stood ready with her unit. Her hands trembled as the orders were given to fire. Running with all her might, she supplied her assigned cannons with powder. Her arms and back ached, but she knew she could not stop. The men depended on her. Emma's legs were shaky and more than once threatened to collapse under her.

During the two-hour barrage of artillery fire, eight-thousand projectiles assaulted Fredericksburg. By the time it was over, all Emma could hear was a loud buzzing sound. Her face was streaked with powder, and her hands burned with new blisters. As the smoke settled, the Union engineers went back to work. From the vantage point on the hill, Emma could barely make out Billy among the men. He had a way of hunching his right shoulder when he was frightened. She squinted as he slipped into the hastily made pontoon and dug his oar into the water.

Against the odds, shots rang out from the devastated town. A strangled cry emerged from Emma's lips as Billy slumped forward and toppled into the cold Rappahannock. Someone next to her ear murmured, "This is madness." The next part of the battle passed in a blur. There were advances across the river and the Confederate troops were confronted and killed. Burnside ordered reinforcements into the town. On the second day of the battle, the Union troops entered Fredericksburg and looted the town.

Emma's mind was racing. Where were Colin and Will? What was happening? She hated the uncertainty of this battle and how they were meant to blindly follow commands, even if it meant death. Days blurred together. Emma's unit entered an artillery battle with Confederate troops. It seemed like men were dying by the thousands before her eyes. Cannon fire blew off legs and arms. She learned to ignore the screams of dying men and carry on, dodging fire herself.

The bloody battle finally came to an end on the evening of December 14th, and the guns fell silent. Accepting tactical defeat, the Union prepared to withdraw to Stafford Heights. Emma and several others picked through the bodies, searching for wounded among the body parts. A hand clawed at her ankle and she forced herself to look down at the blood-stained face of a man. His intestines gaped out of his abdomen.

"Letter...my wife...please."

Emma knelt and groped into his pocket for the precious missive. This process seemed to be repeated too many times for her to count, and she tucked the packet of letters into her pocket. Faintly, Emma heard a familiar voice.

"Take this one! No, not this one. He'll need an amputation."

Emma raised her chin and scrutinized the battlefield, finding Colin directing stretchers. Across the dead and dying, their eyes met. Emma dragged her kepi from her head and sent up a silent prayer to any god still up there. Fighting tears, she replaced her hat, set her jaw, and continued wading through the bodies.

Will groaned, trying to shift the body of another man off his chest. It was insane to keep sending waves of men across an open battlefield. The Confederates had the advantage and picked them off like flies. His fingers sank into the mud as he gritted his teeth. His leg was throbbing rhythmically, and he saw the blood darkening his blue trousers.

"Here! Here!" A young private knelt by him, "Sir, are you okay? Can you hear me?"

Will nodded, grimacing, "My leg."

"Hold on, sir. It's not just your leg. Nasty gash on your head." He waved his arm above his head, "Here, damn it!"

A stretcher arrived and Will was unceremoniously hoisted onto it. The sudden movement caused his eyes to roll back and he slipped into unconsciousness.

"Hold him down, damn it!"

This was hell. Will was sure he had died. No human should be forced to endure this pain.

"Just kill me!" He blurted out.

Someone was lying across his chest. He struggled, but had lost too much blood.

"If you can't hold him, boy, I'll find someone who will!"

"I can! Just do it!"

All reality faded around Will and the last thing he heard were whispered words, "You're going make it, Will. Hang in there. It'll be over soon..."

Emma sat next to Will's cot in the hospital tent. No one

questioned the presence of the young soldier. Several officers inspecting the casualties made little remark to the figure huddled on the stool. Emma's eyes fluttered closed and then she startled awake. Will was pale with a bandage around his head; blood darkened the white fabric. She trailed her eyes down his body to his legs, the right stopping at the knee. Her heart momentarily quickened at the thought of Will going home and living the rest of his life in the bosom of his family.

"Em...I'm thirsty..." Will's scratchy voice had her jumping up out of the chair. She frantically searched for something to give him, as a glass appeared in her hand.

Colin's very empathetic eyes shone down at her. "Here. Slowly."

Emma nodded, tucking her hand behind Will's head and guiding the glass to his lips. He sputtered a bit and Emma's eyes met Colin's. He took the glass and dipped a clean cloth into it. "Dab his lips. It will help for now."

Emma sat on the edge of the bed and did as Colin instructed. Will's eyes fluttered open. He searched hers, as if seeking the answer to a question he already knew. "It's gone, isn't it?"

Fighting tears, Emma looked down and nodded.

Will gazed up at the canvas roof of the tent. "How can I be a husband to Bridget with half a damn leg?"

Emma grasped his cold hand between her own. "She won't care about that! She wants you home, Will. Nothing else matters to her."

Pushing himself up a bit, Will fought the dizziness building in his cloudy head. "You have to go home, Em. If you're found out..." He trailed off as Colin made a slicing motion across his throat.

"Em will be fine, Will. We are hunkering down for the winter. Go home to your family and be thankful."

Will collapsed back on the bed and fell into a fitful sleep. Emma rose and faced Colin, gratitude evident in her eyes.

Colin lamented the lack of sparkle behind those green orbs. She had seen things no man would even fathom in his lifetime. Unable to embrace her, Colin merely pat her shoulder.

"Get some rest, soldier. He'll be transported out in the morning."

"Yes, sir." Emma quickly passed the rows of moaning men, and breathed in the crisp air. Will was going home to Bridget and Wade. Would he keep her secret? She could only hope he would. Emma knew she had to find Harrison, if only she knew where to search.

The winter of 1862 was grim, especially for the Army of the Potomac. Devastated by the Battle of Fredericksburg, men began deserting at a rapid pace. Men were set to guard the perimeter of the camp and shoot any deserter on sight. Morale was at an all-time low. Many of the soldiers were resentful over the dismissal of McClellan. In January 1863, Burnside made a last-ditch attempt to launch some sort of Union offensive against the Confederate forces. The "Mud March" as it came to be known, was a disastrous attempt to gain some upper ground. In the end, two of Burnside's own generals complained to the president, and he was removed from command. There were fears he would drive them to destruction. As 1863 dawned, the Army of the Potomac would have a new commanding officer, Joseph Hooker.

Cold and wet, Emma and her fellow soldiers tried to leach some warmth from the flickering flames. Will had been sent on to a hospital for recovery, and then he would make the final journey back to Rochester. She crept into his tent the night before he left to bid him goodbye, and again he pleaded for her to return as well. There were no punishments for women discovered in the army. They were usually dismissed and sent home. Emma blatantly refused, explaining she was the only one now who could find out where Harrison was, and bring him home.

Colin observed the scene with an impassive expression on his handsome features. Deep in his heart, he still agreed with Will about taking Emma away to safety. This war was going downhill fast. There was no doubt in his mind she would be injured sooner or later. After she departed, he knelt by Will's bedside.

"She is damned stubborn, Col. I do not know how you put up with her mule-headed behavior!" Will slammed his fist into the straw tick mattress.

Colin rocked back on his heels. "I suppose you do pretty crazy things when you are in love."

"Pah! I would be damned to Hell if I let Bridget go gallivanting off to war!"

Rising, Colin began to roll down his sleeves. "That is where you and I differ, Will. I believe in Emma. She has devotion in her heart and when this is over, I hope I get the opportunity to call her my wife. Best of luck, Will."

"Colin?"

The doctor turned and was taken aback by the pain behind Will's eyes.

"Take care of her. Please. If it gets too much, take her out of here and bring her home."

Pressing his lips together, Colin could not deny the man his wish, even though he had already made a similar promise to himself. Shrugging into his greatcoat, Colin maneuvered out of the tent.

Rochester, New York
February, 1863

Rosemarie Mansfield's hands were trembling violently as she held the telegram to her breast. She thanked the delivery boy profusely, resisting the urge to wrap him up in her arms. Scurrying into the parlor, Rose found Bridget with Wade, laughing as the nearly one-year-old pulled himself up on shaky legs, eliciting joyous squeals at his cleverness.

Bridget was momentarily shocked by the breathless entry of her mother-in-law, "Dear Mother Rose, what is the matter? It's not Will, is it?"

Rose answered in the affirmative. "Oh yes, sweet Bridget, but it is not the news we dreaded." She beamed dotingly at Wade, "Your papa is coming home!"

It took a few moments for the words to sink in as Bridget sat wide-eyed. "Will...Will is coming home?"

The slip of paper with the missive handwritten on it was now wrinkled from Rose's tight grasp, but she smoothed it out and handed it to Bridget. She examined the page and began to shake. Throwing themselves into each other's arms, the women hugged and cheered as Wade stared, a mixture of confusion and happiness on his small face.

"What's all this?" William came through the parlor door, having heard the ruckus from the street. Wade held out his chubby arms and was soon scooped up by his beloved grandfather.

Rose held out the paper, "Our Will is coming home!"

William let out a whoop and Wade squealed. "You hear that, young man? Your father is coming home!"

The four hugged and made merry for the rest of the evening, ignoring the sobering reason Will had been discharged. None of them were willing to face the fact their beloved Will would return to them much changed, as the next few days were spent readying a room for Will and Bridget. Rosemarie was unwilling to have them parted from her, and insisted they remain in the house until Will was well enough to go work for his father. Wade chortled with joy and crawled after the women as they wielded dusting cloths and arranged the new room.

Will was adamant he did not need assistance getting back to the house. He wanted to prove even without part of his leg, he was as competent as any other man. Leaning on the wooden crutch, Will limped his way to the door and traversed the steps with caution. Raising a hand, he paused, realizing how silly it was to knock on your own door. Taking a shaky breath, Will turned the handle and called out to the inhabitants.

Rose and Bridget were in the parlor with Wade when they heard the familiar tones echoing through the interior. Racing through the portal, Bridget laid eyes on her husband for the first time in nearly two years. She took in every inch of his form, her gaze lingering on what was left of his leg, before meeting Will's worried look. His eyes were downcast, ashamed of the impression he was leaving on his young wife.

Bridget took a few hesitant steps towards him, caressing his cheek gently, and raising his face to hers. She pressed her lips to his, a tender symbol of her undying love for him, regardless of his injury. Will caught her around the waist and pulled her into a romantic embrace as tears filled Bridget's eyes.

Rose stood in the doorway with Wade on her hip, the boy unsure about the stranger. Placing a hand on Will's back, Bridget guided him over. Rose kissed her son on the cheek and turned the babe to face his father.

"Will, this is your son, Wade."

Will swallowed hard, fighting the rising flood of emotions threatening to overwhelm his person, "Hello, Wade. I am your father."

Wade studied this new man and made the decision he was safe. Reaching out his small hand, he grabbed his father's nose and giggled. The tension was broken and everyone laughed, hugging and rejoicing. Rose bustled her son into the parlor, insisting he rest after his journey. Bridget would not be parted from him, holding his free hand in a vice-like grip. Tea was quickly served with cakes, a luxury saved for such an occasion. After they were fed and warmed, Will began to tell them what happened.

"There are details, my love, that would shock you to the core, and you, Mother, so I will spare them. I was injured at the Battle of Fredericksburg. Thankfully, I survived, found by none other than Doctor Colin McCafferty. He was assigned to the Army of the Potomac. Unfortunately, the sawbones who saw fit to take my leg was neither kind nor understanding. I will not lie, I wished for death."

Bridget gasped. "Thank goodness the doctor was there! And you have healed well?"

Will nodded, drawing his son onto his lap, as the curious toddler decided to explore this new person in his life, "I have. It was a miracle. Many men would not have lived through an amputation...but I had support." Will was reluctant to mention Emma at this point, knowing his family had been through enough with Harrison's sudden departure.

Rose had sent a messenger, as soon as Will arrived, to his father's shop. William burst through the door with all haste. Will struggled to rise as father and son embraced.

"My boy! I was fearful."

"Father...I am here. It will take time to get used to having one leg, but I want to be of use."

William released his eldest son. "There will be plenty of time to discuss those matters. Now, tell me, did you see Emma at the hospital? Is she well? Her correspondence is so sporadic, and only through Mrs. Hastings."

Will sat back down next to his wife. "I will be sure to tell you all I know with haste, Father, but I'm finding myself a bit tired. I think I will go upstairs and rest."

William nodded. "Of course, my boy. Bridget will be happy to have you to herself for a bit, I'm sure." He winked, causing a rosy blush to break out over Bridget's cheeks.

Holding out his hand to his wife, Will allowed her to assist him upstairs, sucking in his pride for her gentle ministrations. Once they were safely ensconced in their room, Bridget gave Will a perceptive tilt of her head.

"You know, do you not, wife?" Will sat on the edge of the bed, drawing her into his arms and resting his head on her breast.

Bridget bestowed a kiss on her husband's head. "Emma is no fool, nor is she heartless enough not to send news home. Where is she, Will?"

Emma Mansfield was at that moment sitting around a fire, well-fed for the first time in many months, having a jovial discussion with several of her fellow soldiers. The smoke wisped upwards to the endless blanket of stars. The new commanding officer, Joseph Hooker, had certainly seen to better accommodations for the men. Morale was high and the men were encouraged after the tragic loss at Fredericksburg. Each soldier was also aware of the momentous Emancipation Proclamation, freeing the slaves. It was rumored many were already enlisting in the Union Army.

Colin and Emma made it a point to meet at least every few days to discuss the war. Since Will left, Colin tried to convince her to go back home. Things were only bound to get worse as time progressed. It did not seem like the Union would win the war.

"I have to find Harrison, Colin, you know this." She angrily whispered to him one evening.

Colin ached to hold her and touch her, but it was impossible. "I know, Em, but what if it is a lost cause? He could be dead already."

"Do not say such things! Harrison is stubborn and would not let this war get the best of him."

"You saw him captured before though. Maybe he is still in a prisoner of war camp. I could find out. I will do what I can to help you, but the minute things get bad, I am taking you out of here. I made a promise to your brother."

Emma narrowed her eyes and spit. Her mannerisms were becoming less ladylike the longer she stayed in the army. She did not respond to his statement, knowing it would be useless to fight his convictions. This was one of the evenings where they would part less amicably than before.

"Too bad Billy is missing this." One of the group remarked and they fell into a sober silence. As much as they had wanted to, recovering Billy's body from the Rappahannock was a fool's errand. Part of Emma hoped he was alive, perhaps washed ashore somewhere. Maybe someone had taken pity and cared for the wounded man. Either way, it was unlikely they would see their good-humored friend again.

"We've lost so many men. It's nigh impossible at this point to think we can win the conflict." Captain Louis Timmons crossed his arms over his impeccably clean uniform. He had been listening to the conversation with vague interest. Timmons commanded a battery of six guns. Emma knew his imposing figure well from the battle at Fredericksburg. He never cracked a smile, and gave orders with strict tones.

"Whaddya mean, Captain?" Richard Bates squared his shoulders, almost insulted that a superior officer would convey such a low opinion of their fighting force.

Captain Timmons, pulling off his hat and running his fingers through his scruffy, reddish-brown hair, refused to meet the eyes of the young man. He appeared to have remembered they were meant to empower, not dishearten, the troops. "I reckon stranger things have happened, Bates."

"The reprieve during the winter months will surely allow the men to recover and come back renewed." Emma spoke softly and low in her throat to disguise her feminine tones.

Timmons glanced up, studying the man who hardly spoke to any superior, except Captain McCafferty. "What did you say, Hawkins?"

Everyone pinned their attention on Emma, who pulled her kepi down a bit lower. "I said, sir, the rest will do us all good."

Replacing his hat, Timmons gave her a curt nod. "You are absolutely correct, soldier." A slip of paper fell from his pocket as he strode away from the group.

Emma quickly stood and called out, "Sir, you dropped something." She retrieved the paper and briefly saw what looked like a battle plan.

Captain Timmons moved swiftly over, snatching it from her. "Did you read this?"

"No, sir." Her heart skipped a beat as Timmons stormed off. A niggling feeling crept into his head about the smooth-faced boy and whether or not he was lying. He roughly pushed past a boy standing at the door of his dwelling.

Emma, shaken by the piercing stare of the captain, retreated to her tent and took up her pen. She still had Billy's letter tucked in her pocket, unable to follow through with her promise to send it on. Pulling out a sheet of paper, Emma smoothed the wrinkles out and applied her pen to the surface.

Dear Aunt,

We have suffered a terrible blow to our forces. Thankfully, I have survived, but I feel a great amount of guilt for it. A friend, Billy, vanished beneath the ripples of the river. I have a letter for his mother, but I do not want to send it. Perhaps he is alive somewhere? I know it is folly to think such.

Many men returned to their families with grievous injuries. I held one officer down while his leg was removed below the knee. I am assured he is back in the bosom of his family, but not after discovering much about my person. I fear I may soon join him before my personal mission is complete.

I am looked after well by a good friend of yours, Doctor McCafferty, who is also aware of much about my person. I know he will keep my confidence.

Much love to all,
Em

Emma folded the letter and addressed it to Mrs. Hastings. She wondered if Will was home and had revealed her clandestine plan to their father. Emma was getting discouraged as it was becoming more and more difficult to find out information regarding Confederate prisoners. She did not want to raise suspicions. Eventually, Emma was resigned to enlisting the help of Colin in her plan.

"I do not think it is a good idea, Em...Private Hawkins." Colin wiped his hands on a towel after rinsing them in the basin by the entry of the hospital tent. He had been making rounds, although the injuries of late were minor.

"Captain McCafferty, it would mean a great deal to my aunt and family if you were able to help me with this request." Em fixed her eyes on his, silently imploring him for some sort of aid, "If they were to know he was safe, I may be able to get back to normal." She stressed the words and hoped he picked up the hints.

Glancing over his shoulder, he hurried her outside and around the back of the tent, "Em, do you mean it?"

"Yes, Colin. I will do what is necessary to ensure I am safely returned." Her voice was low.

Colin straightened as a few men passed, "Very well, Private. I will do my best."

Em saluted appropriately, and vanished back towards the camp of men.

"And that is the entire story, Bridget. She absconded with the assistance of persons unknown, and joined the Union Army." Will dipped his head, ashamed and proud at the same time; a raging conflict of emotions within the young man.

The bed dipped as Bridget sat next to her dejected husband. "I am sure you tried your best to get her to return here to her family, my love."

"I feel like a complete failure to my country, and my family." His brave face completely vanished. Bridget had this uncanny way of eliciting his deepest emotions without even trying.

"My dearest Will, there is no possible way you could ever be a failure in my eyes. It may be selfish, but I am glad you are back and alive. Wade will grow up with a father, instead of a nameless mass grave on a battlefield somewhere unknown." She placed a kiss on his cheek, turning his face towards her with a finger.

Inside Will, his heart melted at the sight of the gorgeous woman beside him, offering him all the love and affection she could muster. “My sweet Bridget, you are more than I could possibly deserve. Wade is an amazing little boy. You have done so well in my absence.”

Bridget feigned offense, “Did you expect any less, you silly man?” She let out a squeal when Will leaned back, deftly pulling her on top of him.

“Never in a million years, my dearest one.” The kisses he lavished upon her were enough to make an innocent maid blush. The talk of Emma was soon forgotten, as the two lovers reacquainted themselves with each other’s touch. Their fervor exploded into sweet murmurs of everlasting promises.

Bridget rested her head on her husband’s bare chest, his strong arms encompassing her petite form. “I pray she is safe and I know she will come back to us.” Her breathing slowed as she slipped into a dreamless sleep.

Will stared at the ceiling for a long time after his wife fell asleep. Her warm body curled against his brought him little comfort. Phantom pains in his amputated lower limb plagued him as much as the haunting thoughts in his head. “If there is a God up there, keep my sister from harm. Do not let her be forsaken like so many others.”

Chancellorsville, Virginia
April/May 1863

Emma stood on the banks of the Rappahannock River, as the soldiers loaded the remaining pontoons and prepared for the cross. She had helped shift the last remaining knee-high barrels of powder, making sure they were tightly sealed. Billy's body had succumbed to the water. She asked later if they had found any sign of her ally and friend. Emma was disappointed with the response. Resigned to the fact Billy was most likely drowned or washed up on some lonely riverbank, she sent his letter onward with her own, full of praise and kind words for the deceased soldier.

Timmons approached the narrow-shouldered artillery soldier and clapped him on the back. Emma nearly stumbled forward from the force of the blow. "Afraid?"

Coughing, Emma shook her head. "No, sir."

"Excellent. We do not need cowards in this army, Hawkins."

Shoulders and spine straightening, Emma took offense to this insinuation. She had remained in a place where braver men had fled. "I am not a coward, sir. I was merely remembering a lost friend. He fell to the mercy of this river during the battle."

Timmons quirked a brow at the elegant speech coming out of the mouth of an apprentice's son. "Where did you say you were from again?"

"New York, sir."

"And...your father was a smith?"

A terse nod was the only reply given.

"You speak very well for a smithy's son." Timmons peered down at the boy.

Emma felt her heart jump into her throat as she formulated a reason for her clipped speech. "My mother, sir, was well-educated. I would be amiss if I did not honor her memory by speaking coarsely."

Timmons seemed to accept this reasoning for the immediate moment. "You sat by Second Lieutenant Mansfield's bed after his leg was chopped off. I remember you."

Emma bit the inside of her cheek. "He was good to the men. They respected him. Again, it would be a disservice not to offer him some comfort, sir."

"You are quite the strange man, Hawkins." Timmons stared out at the rippling waves a few moments longer, before leaving her.

When he departed Emma's side, his presence was replaced by a more familiar figure. "What did Captain Timmons want?"

Emma offered Colin a half-smile. "To throw his weight around, as usual."

"Do you think he suspects..."

Emma cut him off. "Nothing. He's trying to get to know the men under his command. He came around our fire a few nights ago. Probably another means of Commander Hooker working to build morale."

Peering briefly over his shoulder, Colin spotted Timmons watching from several feet away. "You should get back to work."

Emma performed the obligatory salute and returned to her unit. Colin moved back to where they were disassembling the hospital tent. He set about making sure the proper medical supplies were packed away in crates.

While he was kneeling, polished boot toes came into his line of view. "How is it that a doctor spends so much time with a powder monkey?"

Colin slowly rose to his full height, meeting Timmons eye-to-eye. "He is from my hometown. His aunt is a close friend."

Timmons nudged the crate, sending two glass vials clattering into each other with a sickening sound. Colin clenched his teeth. "Watch it. Our boys might need those."

Sneering, the equal-ranked officer thrust his finger into Colin's shoulder. "Stay on your battle lines, sawbones, and keep away from my men. They do not need distraction. We plan to take the Rebs while they are scattered. Don't want some dizzy-headed boy losing track of our objectives."

Colin took the jab in stride. "You have nothing to worry about, Timmons. My care for the boy is nothing more than friendship." He hoisted the crate and took it to a waiting pontoon, leaving the fellow captain seething for reasons unknown.

The last of the pontoons were loaded and lashed down. Emma went to join Bates on the one containing their precious powder when shots rang out. The pair dove for cover as temporary chaos ensued. All was put to rest soon enough when several soldiers dragged forward a pair of men in tattered grey.

As many of the officers were in last minute strategy meetings, the Rebs were brought before Captain Timmons, his bleak, unforgiving stare penetrating the young men slumped on their knees at his feet.

"Well, well! What do we have here? A couple of Reb spies, no doubt! Look too young to be wearing long pants, if you ask me!"

Several of the men guffawed at the joke. In truth, the suspected spies were quite innocent in appearance, despite at least a few days' growth of facial hair.

A snarl emitted from one of the downed men and he leapt up at Timmons, only to be met with a rifle butt to the ribs. Collapsing backwards in pain, his companion remained silent and emotionless. At this point, the crowd of soldiers had grown. Colin pushed his way through the crowd to Timmons' side.

"We do not treat prisoners-of-war in this fashion, Captain Timmons." He leaned down, examining the injured man.

"Self-defense, McCafferty." Timmons smirked, "Put them under guard somewhere, until they can be traded or transported."

Colin rolled back on his heels and rose. "This man has possible broken ribs. He will need to be tended."

Timmons flicked his hand and two privates hoisted the injured Confederate scout, following Captain McCafferty back to his temporary medical unit. Emma watched from a distance as the confrontation unfolded. She did not trust Timmons at all. He was cocky and overly sure of himself. She decided avoiding him would be the best course of action for the remainder of the campaign.

The crossing went as well as could be expected. Knowing Lee's army was waiting on the other side of the Rappahannock caused adrenaline to rise in the veins of the Union artillery unit. The hamlet of Chancellorsville comprised of a rather large field, with a single, brick house perched next to the road. The house had been used as an inn and tavern for many years. It was now occupied by the Chancellor family. The widow and her children stood outside as the Union Army marched in, sassing the opposing troops with great glee. Major General Hooker soon set up the residence as his personal command post.

Emma observed the women and children gather in front of the inn, hoping they would retreat to safety. She knew though they were made of stronger stock, and would hold onto their home as long as possible. Emma and her unit unloaded their pontoons and waited for orders.

"We outnumber these Rebs, Hawkins. No doubt we'll send them back to Richmond with their heads between their legs!" Bates was nearly bouncing with excitement.

Emma compressed her lips together and surveyed the surroundings. They had several advantage points along the Orange Turnpike and the Orange Plank Road. She turned towards the cluster of wilderness enclosing them and a foreboding feeling overcame her body. After nearly a year and a half in battles, Emma was beginning to recognize battle strategy. Although they had already broken through the Confederate brigades guarding the area, Emma knew the untamed wilderness would provide a problem.

"Up there, men! We will have the higher ground." Timmons captured control of his unit and directed them atop a plateau called Hazel Grove. Strategically, it was a prime position for artillery forces. The men began positioning themselves accordingly, laying out powder and ammunition. Emma gave pause to scan the assembling army of nearly 134,000 men. A hand landed heavily on her shoulder.

"Silly to look for him down there, Hawkins. Like finding a needle in a haystack. He'll be with the medical unit a few miles away," Timmons' mocking tone filled her ears.

"I was marveling at the number of men gathered, sir." Emma slipped away to continue her ordered tasks.

By the time evening fell, Hooker had successfully barricaded all roads leading into Chancellorsville. Several preemptive attacks had been made on the Confederate Army's supply lines. Other small operations progressed throughout the last day in April, securing their position. Timmons paced anxiously, a thin, black cheroot between his teeth, as the men tried to rest and put some food into their rumbling bellies.

Emma sat close to Bates, her only trusted companion in the unit since Billy's passing. Neither said a word as they consumed meager rations of salt pork and hard tack. They had fried the hard tack in a bit of grease to prevent it from snapping their teeth. The pair gulped down their watered coffee. Emma's body had hardened due to the poor nutrition and long marches. Patting Bates on the shoulder, she withdrew from the unit for a moment of solitude to write two letters.

Dearest Aunt,

We are at the dawn of another battle and I will openly admit, I am fearful. While we seem to have the advantage, I have little faith in our forces. It sounds so horribly unpatriotic, but the niggling feelings inside me will not rest. Our commanding officer is very certain of his maneuvers, but our unit commander makes me uneasy. If I do not make it out of this engagement, please let everyone know my secret.

Love,
Em

Emma desperately wanted to pen a note to Colin, but if she were found injured, her identity would be compromised. She was resigned to sending up a final prayer, hoping he knew she was thinking of him at this desperate time.

Captain McCafferty tended to his patient, the Confederate scout, and made repeated requests to send him to the bigger hospital. The man had several fractured ribs and Colin feared movement would send the bones into his lung. The pleas fell on deaf ears. There was little sympathy for a man who could reveal their positioning to the enemy. Colin stood by as the scout was unceremoniously hoisted onto a pontoon and ferried across the river like a sack of grain. His face was gritty with dirt; lips chapped raw from lack of fluids.

Colin dipped a clean rag into a bucket and sponged the scout's face. His attention was immediately drawn to the high cheekbones and auburn stubble. Leaning down, Colin murmured into the scout's ear. His eyes immediately snapped open and Colin's speculations were confirmed. It was sheer luck both Mansfield boys had fallen into his lap, so to speak. He knew though the situation of the younger was much direr.

"Do you know what you have done?" Colin hissed, angrily.

A groan emerged from Harrison's lips, the reply stubborn to the end. "I fought for a cause."

"You foolish boy. There is nothing I can do for you now. Either you will die here or find yourself thrown into a prison camp. I do not see either of those doing your condition any bit of good."

Harrison squinted at the man tending him. "Doctor McCafferty?"

Colin shushed him. "Silence. They must not know I know you. We are in Chancellorsville about to engage with Confederate forces. I am...we are...behind the lines."

"Will?"

The sudden worry about his family made Colin more enraged. He wisely bit his tongue. "Sent home after Fredericksburg with half a leg. Quiet now."

The sounds of gun and cannon fire began to erupt in the distance. Colin gave quick orders to set up triage stations and made plans to erect a larger hospital tent. The influx of wounded would be coming soon enough. It was too late and dangerous to seek out Emma at this moment. She would be running back and forth, making sure the cannons were never silent.

Colin let out a breath between his teeth, his heart clenching in his chest. *My sweet Emma, please live to see the end of this. I will find you and we will go home. Your search is over. Just live!*

11

Chancellorsville, Virginia
May 2nd 1863

"He's a completely incompetent commanding officer!" Timmons raged at the cowering artillery corps. The Union had the offensive ground, but Hooker lost his nerve. General Lee was outmaneuvering them, dividing his forces in a bold move, as Hooker watched from his cushy command post at the Chancellorsville Inn. Orders had been given for the artillery to withdraw from the advantageous point at Hazel Grove to Fairview.

"We will be fodder." Timmons muttered, as he ordered the move. Cannons were shifted and Emma began hefting powder bags. By the following morning, four cannons were left as well as approximately 100 men. Confederate forces stormed Hazel Grove.

Bates gave Emma a hard shove towards the retreating men. "Go, Em. Now! This is your only chance!" He held off a few soldiers while she made her way hastily along the path. A bullet whizzed past her, cleanly penetrating the flapping overcoat. The sulphureous stench of black powder hung in her nostrils as she huffed. Every part of her body ached and there was a metallic taste in her mouth. Making it safely to a Union barricade, she glanced back in horror as the Rebs took the men prisoner.

Timmons grasped her by the collar and hauled her back. "You are a coward, Hawkins. Running like hell, while good men are now at the mercy of the Rebels!" He shook her so hard, her teeth rattled in her head.

"Timmons! Enough! He's lucky. We need men to man the cannons here." Another officer scolded the captain who abruptly released Emma. She fell to her bottom in the dirt.

"You're lucky, Hawkins." Timmons kicked a clod of dirt at Emma. She raised her hand defensively, shaking at the confrontation. Scrambling to her feet, Emma made her way to the new artillery line.

The move to withdraw from Hazel Grove gave the Confederate Army a huge advantage. Artillery fire rained down on the fighting Union soldiers. The battle was lost and Hooker ordered retreat back across the Rappahannock. The entire operation was a blur to Emma. The artillery crossed first with Major General Hooker. She caught a momentary glimpse of the man, and disgust filled her throat.

Because of him, her last friend was now captured and would be sent to a vile prison, where he would most likely die of disease or starvation. Many men lay dead and wounded. It seemed no matter who commanded their army, no ground was gained and the mortality rates continued to soar. Upon reaching the opposite bank, the cannons were unloaded and placed strategically to hold the line.

Tears of exhaustion streamed down Emma's face. There was only time for brief periods of rest during the campaign. Her body was weak and aching. Night fell and finally, she was able to rest. The reprieve was short-lived as a hand gently touched her shoulder. Battle wits still about her, Emma reached for her rifle.

"No, Em, it's me." Colin's smiling face entered into view. Emma wanted to throw her arms around him out of utter joy.

"Colin...you're alive." There were dark rings marring her face below her eyes.

Colin repressed the urge to gather her up and spirit her away. "Yes, I am. I was behind the lines. We have not stopped working on wounded for nearly three days. You need to come with me. Now."

Emma did not pause to question the order. Collecting her possessions, she followed on Colin's heels to a tent set apart. There were two guards posted and Colin waved them aside. The inside of the structure smelled dank. The shadowy glow of a lantern revealed two figures, one supine on a hastily made blanket roll and the other hovering close by on his haunches.

"He ain't had nothin' to eat, Doc." The kneeling man confessed, "I've tried, suh."

The Southern tone was mixed with disdain and gratitude, as if the man was confused as to the kind gestures of the doctor. He eyed the young soldier suspiciously.

"Private Hawkins is a family friend. You need not concern yourself, son." Colin dismissed the junior man's worries.

"As you say, suh." He backed away to let the doctor examine the reclining youth, his beady eyes never leaving Emma.

Colin cleared his throat, and gingerly parted the flannel shirt of the injured man. Bandages swathed his torso and Colin cut them away. Even in the dim light, the angry black and blue bruising of his ribs was evident. His rasped breathing filled the tent.

"It has gotten worse. I cannot even get him something for the pain. It's against regulations."

Emma crept closer and quelled her bubbling emotions. The entire time she had been focused on the injury, she had never seized the moment to observe the man's face.

Colin watched her carefully. "You can see the situation is

dire, Hawkins."

"Yes..." Her voice cracked. "I can see that, sir. What can I do?"

"The situation needs time and long-term care. I fear the ribs may be broken." Colin tipped his head down, "They plan to transport these two men in the morning. I believe the care given will not be as...professional during this period."

The cowering scout in the corner of the tent started to cry. "They'll kill us, suh. No doubt."

Colin's face hardened. "Yes, there is that possibility."

"What do we need to do?"

"There are two possibilities. We return the men to the Confederate ranks and pray he gets the proper medical care. Our other option is..."

An argument could be heard erupting at the door to the tent. Timmons' voice clearly echoing above the guards. "One of my soldiers was seen coming this way! I want to know if he was here! Allow me into the tent or I will have you shot for insubordination."

"Captain McCafferty is tending to the wounded man, sir." One of the guards spoke out.

"I do not give a shit what that blue-blood Reb lover is doing. Let me pass!"

Colin held a finger to his lips and motioned to the corner of the tent. Emma crouched low and Colin exited, lantern in hand.

"Timmons, those are some serious charges you have leveled against me. Perhaps we should take this to command?"

"Where is he?" Timmons glared at Colin.

"Control yourself, *Louis*. We are not in the midst of a battle. Your orders and threats mean little at this moment." Colin smirked as he used the informal address.

Teeth gnashed, Timmons squared up to the younger captain. "You look here, I meant it when I said to stay away from my soldiers. I cannot have him wandering around camp when we have a line to defend. Trust me when I say that boy's life will be a living Hell when I get a hold of him."

"You will have to look elsewhere, Timmons. Your powder monkey is not here." Colin planted his feet firmly. Timmons raged, but stalked off. Colin let out a breath and thanked the guards. Timmons had gathered up a rather unsavory reputation, and many found his actions reprehensible towards some of the young men. Colin waited until he was well out of sight before ducking back into the tent.

Emma's fearful eyes met his in the lantern light.

"We leave tonight." Colin turned on the second scout. "Listen to me good, son. If you want to see the light of day again, you will help us. I can get you back to the Confederate forces, but you must never breathe a word to anyone. If you do, your friend will surely die. Do you understand?"

Confused by the situation, but unwilling to give up an opportunity to escape back to his lines, the scout agreed. "What's gonna happen to him?"

"He will live. That is all you need to know. This young man here will help me. Do you trust us?"

"Suh, as a doctor, I trust you, but not as a Yank. For him though, I'll do it." He gestured to the man on the bedroll. "I pray to God you'll make it out alive."

"You have to hit me. Hard. Slip out the back of the tent using this knife and run to the river. It's not far." He handed the blade to the scout, "Hawkins, you raise the alarm. Follow him out of the tent. You've been on a walk. Am I clear?"

Emma nodded, marveling at Colin's quick thinking. She heard what Timmons said. No doubt he would be her undoing in the unit. She winced as the sickening thud of knuckles to jaw reached her ears. Colin slumped to the ground, stunned. The scout gave her one hesitant glance before slicing through the canvas of the tent and slipping into the darkness.

Casting a concerned look back at her love, Emma fled the tent after the scout. She allowed him a head start to the bank of the river before calling out, "Escape! The prisoner has escaped!"

Her cries broke the silence of the night and the camp came alive. Orders were swiftly given and men began to pursue the fleeing Confederate. Emma turned to head back to the tent and ran straight into Timmons, who hoisted her up by the collar. The action was turning into his common greeting for her.

"You! How do I know you did not aid the escape?" His breath was thick with whiskey fumes, and she nearly fainted at the smell.

"I...I...was walking and I saw him running to the riverbank, sir!" She managed to squeak out, his fist pressing into her throat.

"I will deal with you later." Emma found herself thrust to the ground, as Timmons went off to help organize the recapture of the scout.

Momentarily stunned, Emma sat in the dirt for a few crucial minutes, before returning to the scene of the planned escape. Colin was rubbing his jaw. "A few officers came and went. I assured them I was well enough to stay guarding a wounded man."

Emma did not care who saw them at this point. She catapulted herself into Colin's arms and nestled her face into his neck. They embraced for a few precious moments as the noises in the camp faded from awareness. Holding her at arm's length, Colin brushed away the tears streaking down her dirty cheeks.

"We do not have a great deal of time if we want to get your brother out of here." As much as he wanted to continue touching her slim form, Colin knew action must be taken. "A supply wagon is our best bet."

Emma swallowed hard and nodded, composing herself before slipping out of his grasp and searching for the required conveyance.

Colin turned back to the man on the pallet. "Can you hear

me? We are getting you out of here."

A groan was the only reply he garnered from the injured man. The sound of hooves approaching let Colin know Emma had been successful in retrieving a cart. With her careful aid, they negotiated Harrison out of the tent. His pale coloring was worrisome. Emma noticed how frightfully innocent her younger brother seemed. Emma climbed into the back of the covered wagon and drew his head into her lap. His eyes flickered open, but no recognition passed before them, as Colin clicked his tongue and tapped the reins against the horse's back.

The fleeing party set off away from the river. Their best chance of escaping was to circumvent the military lines of both sides and get into the woods off the beaten path. As they bounced along, Harrison beseeched Emma for some water. Colin directed her to dampen a cloth and press it to his lips, as she had done with Will.

Brushing his hair back, Emma cradled her brother, wondering how he came to this. Since she spotted him on the supply run, his face had thinned considerably. Although two years her junior, Emma and Harrison had been close. Will never could relate to his youngest sibling, finding him more a nuisance than playmate. Harrison would run to Emma if he hurt himself horsing around in the garden. It pained her they had grown apart as each moved toward adulthood. As the wagon rattled onward, Emma hoped he would survive the strident journey ahead of them.

Rochester, New York
June, 1863

Elizabeth Hastings was rarely fearful of anything life threw in her path. She had helped Emma willingly, hoping the girl would gain some knowledge, and return without further incident. Quite sure her role as accomplice went unknown,

Mrs. Hastings began to relax and organize her war-time efforts. As she sat at her writing desk, basking in the warm afternoon sun reflecting through her window, Millie entered the parlor.

"Mrs. Hastings, there is a Mrs. Bridget Mansfield at the door. Were you expecting her?"

"No, dear Millie, but show her in. We cannot be too sociable in times like these." Mrs. Hastings straightened, bringing a hand to her bun and tucking in any loose strands of snow-white hair.

Bridget entered the parlor with apologies. "Mrs. Hastings, I know I should have informed you of my visit in advance."

"Nonsense, my dear. Do sit." She directed her guest to a chaise and joined her, "How is your delightful son?"

Bridget wrung her hands, portraying the picture of a demure lady. "Oh, he is very well and thriving. Will and I never tire of his antics." She drew in a breath. "If I may, I will get to the point of my visit. Will revealed some information to me, even though I was already aware something was amiss. I seek your advice on the matter."

"Oh? Do go on." Mrs. Hastings quickly asked Millie for some refreshment, and the maid retired from the parlor.

"Yes, you see, Will encountered Emma during his time in the army and, I am afraid to say, she was not nursing wounded men."

Feigning shock, Mrs. Hastings brought a hand to her breast. "My goodness!"

Bridget leaned in. "Do not play the fool with me, ma'am. I can think of no one Emma admired more, and would turn to for help if she chose to enter the ranks of the army."

Mrs. Hastings' face hardened. "If you are asking me to admit if I am Emma's accomplice, well, my dear, I simply cannot do that."

Bridget stood. "You do not have to, ma'am. I am shocked you would even consider putting Emma in danger, regardless of the reason."

"Emma makes her own choices, Mrs. Mansfield. I can assure you of her safety. I highly doubt Doctor McCafferty would see her come to harm."

"And if he fails to act as the white knight?"

Millie rapped on the door of the parlor and entered. "Pardon me, ma'am, but this telegram just arrived for you."

Mrs. Hastings rose and took the missive from Millie, her brows creasing as she read. "Oh my!"

Bridget approached and glanced at the paper. "Emmett Hawkins, listed as a deserter. Report all activity to the Union Army, under penalty of criminal charges."

Folding the paper, Mrs. Hastings tucked it away into her writing desk. "It seems we have much bigger worries now."

Dumfries, Virginia
Late May, 1863

The unseasonable cold almost burned Emma's cheeks, bringing a ghostly pallor to her skin. Her breath formed misty clusters of white, as she shrank down deeper into her wool overcoat. Her lips were chapped, as the frost ripped all moisture from the black night. Letting her head rest against the rough bark of the willow tree, Emma waited for Colin to return. They had not risked a fire, and the night air was beginning to seep through her clothing. The trio had long abandoned the uniforms of their respective armies for less conspicuous clothing.

Clutching her rifle close, Emma chanced closing her eyes, when the sound of a twig snapping broke the bitter silence and her momentary peace. Her body tensed and breath escaped her lungs. She peered out into the darkness. Suddenly, hands clamped around her, one gloved hand cupped over her mouth.

Before Emma could scream or struggle, Colin's soothing voice filled the hollow of her ear, "Stand and move back. I was followed."

Emma nodded and he released her. She soundlessly picked up her canvas bag and the rifle. The grass whispered beneath the soles of her boots, as she traced Colin's shadow. There was no more than a sliver of moonlight.

They had hidden Harrison amongst a crop of trees, wrapped in the canvas stripped from the wagon. Emma tugged Colin's sleeve. "We should not have given up the horse."

"It drew too much attention." He handed her a rope. They managed to fashion a sort of stretcher with the materials. "I found a hunting cabin not far from here. We can rest tomorrow, and plot a reasonable path back."

As they trudged through the underbrush, every noise gave them both pause. Emma's heart was beating hard and fast in her ears. By the time they made it to the cabin, Emma was sure her head would burst. There was a thick layer of dust on the floor, indicating no one had resided there in quite some time. Colin flicked a match and the light illuminated the interior. A rickety bed perched in the corner, covered in a straw tick mattress. A stone fireplace, blackened from many fires, occupied one wall. There was a small table and two chairs with cupboards hanging open. It seemed someone had already tried to raid the cabin for food.

"Help me get him onto the bed." Emma and Colin hoisted Harrison onto the straw mattress. He emitted a low moan, as Colin checked him over.

"Thankfully, he is getting better. I am sorry to say, we cannot risk a fire."

Emma gave him a shaky smile. "I understand."

Colin crossed and wrapped his arms around her trembling body. "It will be fine, Emma. I promise." He pressed his lips to her brow.

Harrison blinked a few times in the dim light. "Where am I?"

Emma knelt by his side. "You are in a cabin in the woods outside of Chancellorsville, Harrison."

"Emma? What on Earth are you doing here? What happened to your hair?"

Laughing, Emma gazed up at Colin, "Of all the things to worry about, and he asks what happened to my hair!"

A loud pounding on the door interrupted their revelry. Colin shushed them immediately and gestured to Emma. He positioned himself behind the door.

Emma doffed her hat and opened the portal. A woman in a woolen shawl and patched dress stood before her.

"Sorry to bother you, miss...it is 'miss'?"

Emma eyed her warily. "What do you need?"

She peered past Emma into the cabin. "I thought so. Don't like them Yanks or the Rebs. Thought you should know, they're combin' the woods." She thrust a brown paper package into Emma's hand. "Bread and a bit of salt pork. God bless."

Pulling the shawl up around her head, the woman vanished into the night. Emma eased the door shut and bit her lower lip. Colin placed a hand on her shoulder.

"Nothing we can do, Emma, until the morning."

Harrison struggled to sit up, sucking his breath between his teeth. Colin hurried over. "No, you need to be as still as you can. A rib might puncture your lung."

"They certainly hit me hard enough. Not surprised." He fixed a stare on Emma. "Do I want to know why my sister is here?"

Emma knew her appearance was not what her youngest brother expected to see. "I came after you and Will. Will was listed as missing. He's well though, and back home with the family. You're an uncle. Bridget bore a baby boy, Wade." Emma bit her tongue. What she wanted to do was give him a right scolding for the hell he had put their parents through with his behavior.

Harrison faced away from her. "I know what I did was silly, Emma. I regret every moment. I was headstrong, and unable to accept reason."

Colin observed the siblings in sober silence. Traversing wilderness, as well as avoiding roaming patrols of both Union and Confederate soldiers with an injured man, seemed to be a nigh impossible task. Letting the horses go was a mistake. He rubbed the bridge of his nose and took a seat at the ramshackle table, Emma's soft voice becoming background to his worries.

After nearly an hour of reminiscing, Harrison grew tired and drifted off to sleep. Emma rose and approached Colin, placing her hands on his shoulders. "He feels so poorly about his actions. He's been captured once before. It must have been when I saw him in Cumberland. He was traded back with a few other men in place of a Union officer."

Colin made a noise. "Hmm."

Emma circled him, and sat in the other chair. "What is it, my love?"

The endearment melted Colin's concerns away for a brief moment. "Emma, you know we have to make it back to Rochester. They will be looking for us though. Who knows when this war will end? Your best bet might be to carry on without me. If I go back now, the worst I will suffer is demotion."

Emma nodded, sadness sweeping her face. "As much as I hate to say, you must. Timmons will no doubt have raised the alarm and be looking for me."

"There is little honor in leaving you and Harrison to fend for yourselves."

"You will do better for us by being a helping hand on the outside."

Colin grasped Emma's hands in his and kissed her narrow fingers. "My sweet Emma, it breaks my heart to leave you again so suddenly. In the morning, I will take you out and we will get some supplies. You can stay at this cabin for a few weeks before moving on."

Emma sighed softly. "You can always say we took you by force. You would be blameless then."

Caressing her cheek, Colin shook his head. “I cannot. It would mean you might be shot, or jailed, for your crimes. No, my darling love, I must go back to keep you safe, and pray I live to the end of this war.”

Rochester, New York
Late May, 1863

Bridget and Will sat in the parlor, deep in private conversation, as Wade played with carved wooden blocks at their feet. Rose gently rapped at the open door and entered, carrying a tea tray. As the war continued, middle- and upper-class families realized they would have to begin assisting in their own households, as more and more men went off to battle. She set the service on a table and opened her arms to Wade, who toddled over to give his grandmother a hug.

Settling the small boy on her lap, Rose addressed the couple. “I do apologize for interrupting your time together, but I thought you would like some tea. Dinner will be late tonight.” Wade eagerly snatched a rare cake from the tray, sugar covering his small face.

Will patted Bridget’s hand, trying to banish the worried countenance from her face. “We would love tea, Mother. Thank you kindly.”

Rose frowned, delicate lines forming around her eyes. “Will, what is it? Something is wrong, I know that much.” She silenced denials with a simple raised palm. “William, a mother knows. Please tell me.”

The pair shared a worried glance before Will began to speak. “Mother, as you know, I served with the Army of the Potomac during my time with the Union forces. While I was there, I met a youth by the name of Emmett Hawkins. He was a private with the artillery forces, low on the chain, but a very hard worker.”

Rose inclined her head, "Do go on, Will. Has this young man befallen some sort of misfortune?"

Will seemed unable to go on, so Bridget continued, "In a manner of speaking, Mother Rose. Emmett Hawkins is listed as the nephew of our own Mrs. Hastings."

"Gracious! I did not know she had living relatives."

Will's hand tightened around Bridget's, finding strength in her presence. "That is just it, Mother. Mrs. Hastings does not."

"Who is this Emmett Hawkins then? Surely not some imposter taking advantage of the goodwill of Mrs. Hastings?" Wade slipped from Rose's lap to take back up with his blocks.

"Not exactly, Mother. You see, Emmett Hawkins is not exactly a young man."

Rose's expression darkened and Will could see his mother's mind working to deduce the riddle. "You had better tell me, Will, although I do fear the worst now."

"Emmett Hawkins is actually our dear Emma."

Eyes flying wide open, Rose clasped a hand to her breast. This was clearly not what she was expecting to hear, as she fanned herself wildly with her free hand. "You cannot mean...oh my dear stars!"

Bridget immediately went to her side, comforting her gently. "There, there, Mother Rose."

"My daughter! Amongst all those men! She will be ruined, surely!"

Will leaned forward slightly, "Mother, there is more."

"More? What more can there possibly be? Doctor McCafferty will never have her now!" The panic showed no signs of ebbing in her tone.

"Mother! Listen! Doctor, rather, Captain McCafferty knows. He assured me at the first sign of danger to her person, he would turn her around and send her back to us. Her honor is more than safe."

Rose clutched Bridget's hand. "Where is she though?

Why did she not come home with you?"

Will exhaled sharply. "She wants to find Harrison. She refused to come back until she knew if he was safe or not."

Rose paled considerably and her eyes fluttered back, slumping into a faint. Bridget cried out. Her mother-in-law was not weak-hearted. Will sat anxiously, quite helpless to move to his mother's aid. Bridget frantically fanned, and tapped, her cheeks until she came round.

"Mother Rose! Thank goodness! I was worried we were going to have to send for a doctor."

Rose fiddled with the collar of her dress, releasing the first button in an attempt to get more air. "You must not breathe a word of this to your father."

"On that, Mother, I do believe we can all agree. The only thing we can do now, is wait for news of her safety."

Dumfries, Virginia
Late May, 1863

Emma and Colin rose early, having slept on bedrolls in front of the cold fireplace. Colin woke periodically throughout the night to check on Harrison, who seemed to be improving now he knew Emma was taking him home. The pair left Harrison sleeping, and traveled a short distance away to see about supplies and meat for the journey. The morning air was pleasant with sunbeams creeping through the treetops. For a moment, they forgot where they were, and enjoyed their last morning together.

Emma smiled warmly at Colin, as they returned to the cabin. A horse whinnying stopped them dead in their tracks. Colin drew Emma back behind some shrubs, on a small hill overlooking the cabin. A pair of horses stood outside the open door, a private dressed in blue stood holding their reins. A wave of helplessness consumed Colin as he watched, knowing exactly what was happening.

A loud commotion erupted from the interior of the cabin. Emma lunged forward, but Colin snagged her around the waist, drawing her head into the crook of his neck. Two shots rang out and Emma smothered a scream into Colin's shoulder as she broke down. Colin's eyes narrowed as Captain Timmons exited the cabin with a smoking Colt revolver. He was closely followed by a private, whose face was as white as a ghost.

"They cannot be far. You should start combing the woods. I want the boy and Captain McCafferty found, and brought to me alive, you hear?" He mounted the horse. "I will be back at camp." He trotted off through the underbrush.

The two privates stared at each other in disbelief. Their captain had murdered an unarmed man in his bed. They scanned the neighboring trees as Colin desperately tried to keep Emma calm. Both knew what had transpired in the cabin. Harrison was surely dead, and Colin could not leave Emma alone to fend for herself. He settled her as the privates stood, dumbfounded, and unsure of where to start their search. By mid-afternoon, they finally departed in silence.

Colin crept down towards the cabin, Emma in his arms. Exhaustion overtook her and she slept restlessly. A stick snapped and he spun, finding himself face-to-face with the pair of soldiers.

"Captain..." One of them stepped forward. "We need to take you back to camp. Everyone is in an uproar."

The second rubbed his eyes as he observed the sleeping person in Colin's arms. "Wait a second...that's Hawkins! But...what happened to him? He's got..." The boy blushed vivid scarlet.

"You know this soldier?"

The private nodded. "Name's Richard Bates, sir. We served together. The captain thought I would be best to go after him, sir."

"Bates, we need to clear the cabin. I cannot bring...this soldier into it the way it is."

Bates' companion was torn between loyalty and disgust for Captain Timmons. "We should...we could get into real trouble, sir."

Colin was growing frustrated. "Then I will do it. Get me a bedroll for Hawkins."

Bates complied, still in awe at the transformation of his companion. "Sir, is Emmett Hawkins...I mean to say, is he actually a woman?"

Laying his tender burden on the blankets, Colin faced Bates. "Yes, but you must, you both must, never breathe a word of her existence in the Union Army."

Colin left the pair outside as he entered the cabin. The familiar metallic smell of blood assaulted his nostrils as he lit a lantern. Harrison was slumped out of the bed, his foot caught on the blanket. There was a bullet hole in his chest and one in his head. Colin ran his fingers through his hair. Poor man never stood a chance. He reemerged and gestured to Bates.

"I doubt Union forces will return for the body. We need to bury him and give him the respect he deserved."

"Who is he, sir?"

Colin sat next to Emma's sleeping form, and rested his head in his hands. "Someone should know the story, I suppose, if something should happen to us." He proceeded to reveal the Confederate soldier, Harrison Mansfield, to be the brother of Will and Emma Mansfield, also known as Emmett Hawkins. Colin explained he had sworn to Emma's brother, a second lieutenant in the Union Army, he would bring Emma back safely, even at the expense of his own rank.

Bates' mouth hung open as Colin concluded the story. His companion frowned deeply, but said nothing.

"So, you see, the respectful thing to do is to lay this man to rest as fitting a soldier. It does not matter what side we fight for. All of us fight for a cause we believe in. It does not make either of us right, or wrong."

They slowly digested his words before nodding. Bates spoke up for the two of them. "We will help, Captain, because I know you are an honorable man. Timmons shot a man in cold blood, without a fair trial. That is not right."

Together, the men managed to dig a shallow grave in the fragrant earth. Colin wrapped Harrison's body in a sheet, unable to even take a memento, as the man had none. They lowered his body into its final resting place, and covered him. The sun was beginning to set.

"I don't know many prayers, Captain." Bates seemed humbled by the ritual.

A feminine voice came from behind them. "Harrison did not care much for religion. He went to church out of respect for our parents."

The men parted as Emma came forward. "Hawk...Miss Mansfield." Bates bobbed his head.

Emma was not fazed by the new address. "Hello, Private Bates. This was so kind of you."

"We should say something, Emma." Colin drew her to his side.

Emma nodded, "Yes, I know." She held up a slim volume of poetry and opened to a creased page, her voice echoing clear in the cool evening.

"After the Battle by Thomas Moore.

Night closed around the conqueror's way,
And lightnings show'd the distant hill,
Where those who lost that dreadful day
Stood few and faint, but fearless still.
The soldier's hope, the patriot's zeal,
For ever dimm'd, for ever crost –
Oh! who shall say what heroes feel,
When all but life and honour's lost?

The last sad hour of freedom's dream,
And valour's task, moved slowly by,
While mute they watch'd, till morning's beam
Should rise and give them light to die.
There's yet a world, where souls are free,
Where tyrants taint not nature's bliss; --
If death that world's bright opening be,
Oh! who would live a slave in this?"

Somewhere in West Virginia
July, 1863

Emma's shirt stuck to her back as they traversed the wilderness, staying off the main roads. A little over a month had elapsed since they left Harrison buried in the woods, and sent the two privates back to camp with nothing to report. Their loyalty to Emma shocked Colin, but he realized, even through her façade as a male, she had been able to garner the respect and admiration of her compatriots.

While on a covert trip into a small town for supplies, Colin picked up some murmurs of a great battle in Pennsylvania, at Gettysburg. It was a Union victory, but with many casualties on both sides. Emma's tears fell anew when he told her. She confessed her worry for her friends in the artillery unit. A wave of shame and guilt swept over both of them, each knowing they could have made a small difference.

Colin collected a newspaper on his visit and read the article aloud, the reporter heralding the battle a turning point for the Union forces. "Just think, a little over a year ago, all hope seemed lost."

The crickets echoed a chorus through the woods, as Emma watched the smoke from the fire spiral upwards to the clear, night sky. The night was warm, and their bellies were full for the first time in a matter of weeks. Avoiding roaming patrols was becoming easier and, with the conflict at Gettysburg, they knew why.

"How long do you think it will all last?" Emma scooted closer to Colin, nestling into his side.

Colin wrapped an arm around her, kissing the top of her head. Emma's auburn hair was slowly growing back, as she saw no need now to keep it shorn. It fell in delicate waves to her jaw. "I do not know, my love."

In the gentle glow of the firelight, it was easy to forget the turmoil of the world around them. Emma tilted her head and placed a kiss on Colin's jaw. "Thank you for coming with me. I know I act brave, but I was really terrified."

Colin squeezed her softly to his side. "I am sure there were simpler ways to get you home."

"Timmons will be looking for me. Even if I did make it, he may go after Mrs. Hastings. This is much safer because she doesn't know where I am."

"Do you think he would go as far as to track down your family in New York?" Colin's brow creased.

Emma threw another log onto the fire. "I am absolutely certain of it. He had some sort of sore spot for me. Perhaps he took my silence as defiance."

"War makes even civil men savage."

Emma contemplated his words for a few silent moments. The comradery she experienced among many of the common soldiers was something different than the stilted conversation and mannerisms of officers. Her thoughts were interrupted by Colin's lips caressing her jawline.

"Since our first night together, not a day has passed where I haven't dreamed of holding you naked in my arms."

Emma shivered, even in the warmth of the fire. "Colin,

would you even conceive of speaking to me in this manner, were we courting properly at home?"

His breath was warm on her ear, as he whispered, "Back home, I would not have already had the pleasure."

"That is simply shocking, my darling." Emma turned her body towards him and succumbed to his ardent kisses. Perhaps the strain of the last weeks was finally beginning to melt away from her, as she lay in his fervent embrace.

Colin ran the pad of his thumb over her delicate features. "Life will be so much simpler after this war. We will marry, have children, and love each other until the very end of our days."

The lustrous orange and red flames reflected in his eyes, the ones Emma had stared so deeply into the night of the Christmas social. The evening of revelry seemed so far in the past and she wondered if she even resembled the woman Colin beheld with such impassioned reverence. She brushed back a bit of his hair, overgrown from the lack of a barber's care.

"Colin, do you still love me as much as you did the first night we realized our feelings?"

Colin tilted her chin up and claimed her mouth, whispering huskily against her lips. "My brazen love, what do you think?"

"If it is even possible, I am more in love with you than ever."

"You have your answer." His kisses made her knees feel weak, as they let the world of war and chaos slip to the back of their minds in a hazy mist. Honor and duty meant nothing to either of them at that exact moment. With zealous pleasure, Emma and Colin rekindled their lust for each other, first experienced in the small space of a canvas tent.

Colin's hands skimmed over her skin, still soft despite the bitter circumstances. The curves of her elegant form warmed to his touch, his breath catching in his throat as she unbuttoned her shirt, baring the silky, rounded breasts which so haunted his dreams. Their coupling was not rushed, but tender, with moments of unbridled devotion. Their cries of delight rose into the air when Colin finally entered her warm sheath. Emma gripped his muscular shoulders as she rode his thrusts, meeting each with sweet cries of sensuality. The night calm broke with mutual moans of satisfaction. Colin enfolded Emma in his arms and cradled her head against his chest.

Front Royal, Virginia
July, 1863

The Battle of Gettysburg had concluded with a clear Union victory. The Army of the Potomac occupied the town of Front Royal, having cut off the retreating Confederate forces through the Manassas Gap, but plans of pursuit were disbanded after reinforcements arrived. The Confederates withdrew into the Luray Valley, but the Union foothold was secure. This would be the last time General Lee would launch an offensive against the Union. Major General George Meade was now in charge of the Army of the Potomac, and harshly criticized for allowing Lee's army to evade capture a second time.

Captain Louis Timmons' focus was momentarily on other matters, as he assessed the damage to his artillery corps. Many men perished in the battle and still more were wounded. One medical officer made the near-fatal mistake of mentioning Captain McCafferty in his presence and wound up with a broken nose. Timmons' inability to track McCafferty and Hawkins irritated him to no end. Coming through the battle with only a mild head laceration was little consolation.

Pacing his tent, Timmons gave momentary pause to allow his wound dressing to be changed. His head throbbed from the injury as his rage intensified. Private Bates earned himself strenuous cleaning duties for his inability to produce the captives alive. The man seemed fiercely loyal to his former compatriot, refusing to give detail of the events after Timmons rode off. It was clear, though, he was disgusted by the actions of shooting an unarmed man, even a Reb.

When Timmons reported back the outcome of his excursion to find the fugitives, his superiors were less than pleased. The brow-beating he received intensified his desire to see McCafferty and Hawkins shot. Faced with suspicion over the death of the Confederate scout, yet unable to prove any wrongdoing on the part of the captain, left Timmons with an ever-present black cloud circling around him. There was no denying the murmurs of excessively forceful behavior as he surveyed the soldiers under his command.

Sitting on his cot, Timmons gingerly touched the clean bandage over his wound. It made little difference to him what the other men thought. His life to this point had been more hellish than they could imagine. There was no conceivable way he was going to be beaten by a skinny kid and a well-meaning captain. His resolve hardened, Timmons swore on his first available leave date he would be paying a visit to a certain aunt in New York. Reclining back, a smile formed on his face. Yes, the key to getting to the boy, would be to destroy the woman.

The embers of the fire had long dimmed as the dawn broke. Colin, content to remain warm in Emma's arms, knew they must be moving, on lest they be discovered. Shaking his beloved awake, he rose to dress and stoke the fire, to cook some salt pork in fat for their breakfast. Emma stretched, and threaded her fingers through her hair, trying to restore some semblance of order to the tangled tresses. The image was more than enough to make the blood rise in Colin's body. He quelled his urges for now, offering her a morning greeting and smile.

Emma tucked the blanket around her, as she sought out her discarded garments. “Where are we headed from here?”

“We should get closer to the Appalachian Mountains. It will be safer for us, and we can follow them north. Crossing through Pennsylvania may be a bit treacherous, but we will make it.” Colin unfolded a map out of his bag. It was creased, and tearing at the edges.

“You were very prepared for our journey.” She eyed him suspiciously.

Colin rocked back on his haunches. “Would you hate me if I told you I have been ready to flee with you for some weeks, since Will left? Harrison...well, his capture was just fortuitous, and gave me the reason I needed.”

Emma lowered her eyes, hugging her knees. “Timmons did not need to shoot him. Harrison was only a boy.”

“Emma, I am so sorry I could not do more to protect your brother. It is my greatest regret.”

Placing her arms through the shirt sleeves, Emma began to do up the buttons. “Harrison knew what he was getting into when he ran away...at least, it is my fondest hope he did.”

Colin knew Harrison most likely took little stock in the consequences of his actions. His impulsiveness drove his decisions, but Colin was unwilling to break his true opinions on the matter to Emma. Instead, he gave a curt nod, and continued studying the map, tracing his finger along the surface.

“Colin, do you miss your father?”

The question came suddenly and Colin found himself unprepared. “Why do you ask?”

Emma sought out the homespun trousers and slipped them over her legs, tucking in the shirt, before sitting by the fire. “You rarely speak of him. Did you write him letters as you did me?”

Colin brought over a tin plate of food to Emma and knelt

beside her. "Things between my father and I are very complicated. I wish him no ill fate, but we simply do not speak. It has been that way since I left for medical school. While he was happy to support my education, I believe part of him was reluctant."

"Do you believe he would want to hear of you...of us? Surely it would be an opportunity to mend broken bonds?"

"I will consider it, my love. Now, please eat. We have to make some headway before the sun gets too high." The conversation subject was firmly closed. Breaking camp, Emma and Colin hefted their bags and began their advance to the mountains.

14

Rochester, New York
August, 1863

Wade raced down the stairs, belly first, much to the shock and horror of his mother. The precocious toddler adventured and climbed everywhere, taking advantage of the large yard area with glee. The summer months brought warm weather, and much time spent outdoors. Will lamented he could not chase Wade as fathers should, and took to watching him from the covered porch. Wade was a delight to many of the neighbors and a hope for a stronger next generation as reports flowed in daily of the missing, wounded, and dead.

On this particular morning, Bridget descended the stairs rapidly after her son, the boy having heard a knock at the door. Wade was particularly keen on discovering new guests arriving at the residence, and demanding to be carried about, drawing all the attention to his chubby face. Bridget waved off the maid and opened the portal herself, scooping Wade up to balance on her hip. She smiled graciously at the messenger boy, shifting from foot to foot in her presence.

"May I help you?"

"Yes ma'am. I'm lookin' for ummm, Mister...umm...Second Lieutenant Mansfield?" The boy doffed his hat, and twisted it between his hands.

"I am his wife. He is resting at the moment. May I help you?" She jiggled the toddler, ignoring his protests to be released.

"You see, ma'am, I was sent here to ask him some questions, please, ma'am. If I go back without the right answers, he'll skin me alive! Pardon my language, ma'am." The poor boy was so nervous, Bridget thought he was going to drop to the floor in a faint.

"Why not come in and I will see if I can get him to come speak to you." Bridget gestured to a waiting maid, and she ushered the scruffy-faced boy into the parlor. Bridget watched for a moment before ascending the stairs. She rapped on her mother-in-law's door and beseeched her to keep Wade occupied, before scurrying down the hall to their own room.

Will was sitting up on the bed, studying some of the store accounts. He smiled warmly as his beloved wife came in, but the happy expression slipped from his face. "What's wrong?"

Bridget wrung her hands. "There is a young boy here to see you. He says it is very urgent he speak to you in person. It seems he was sent by someone."

Will shifted himself to the side of the bed and took up his crutches, shunning all help from his wife. Although slightly hurt, Bridget was used to the slight. Will was still determined not to be a burden. She descended the stairs ahead of him, turning to make sure he was able to traverse the steps. Once at the bottom, she brought him into the parlor, where the youth stood nervously by the cold fireplace.

Will maneuvered himself to one of the sofas and sat, placing the crutches at his side. Bridget stood by the door. Will cleared his throat. "Well, speak up. What is this urgent message?"

The boy turned, and eyed the missing limb with shock. "Did that happen...?"

"Fredericksburg. Now, come out with it. You did not come to my home to ask about an amputated limb." Will was unused to being the object of attention. His missing limb drew many stares and comments. People hailed him a hero, but he did not see it.

"Sorry, sir. I was sent here to ask you about Private Hawkins, sir. You see, he's missin', and the captain wants to know why. Seems he spent a lot of time with yourself?" The boy was extremely uncomfortable with this task, and shuddered fearfully.

Will forced himself to relax at the mention of his sister's fake name. "What's your name, son?"

"Benjamin Taylor, sir."

"And this captain?"

"Captain Timmons, sir." The boy shuddered again.

Will glanced up at Bridget, his brow wrinkled in concern. "Benjamin, who is Captain Timmons to you?"

Benjamin twisted his cap so hard, Bridget thought the fabric was going to tear. "He caught me, sir, trying to steal some food. You see, my pa, he was killed, and my ma and sister were starvin'! He said if I worked for him, he'd give me food."

"And did he keep his agreement?" Will's skepticism found its way into his tone.

Benjamin shook his head. "No, sir. He said he knew where my ma and sis were, and he would kill them if I didn't do exactly as he said. He sent me up here for the truth, and I'm not to leave until I get it, sir."

"I am afraid, Benjamin, you will be very disappointed. I do not know Private Hawkins apart from our interactions on the battlefield. He saved my life and made sure I recovered from my injury, as so many other men did not. You will need to report that to Captain Timmons. I can sign a statement to that effect, should you wish?"

Crestfallen, Benjamin nodded. "He'll be sending me to that old lady's house next."

Bridget approached the boy. "Of which old lady might you be speaking?"

"He said we had to see her while he was on leave. Her name is...oh darn...pardon me, ma'am. She's a widow lady, you see."

Bridget's lips formed a fine line. "Mrs. Hastings?"

"That's it, ma'am!"

Bridget shot Will a knowing look before placing her hand lightly on the boy's back. "Why don't you..."

Benjamin let out a yelp and jumped a foot into the air. Bridget's hand flew to her breast.

"What on God's Earth?"

Will leaned forward. "Come here, Benjamin." His tone was kind, but firm. The boy hesitated before approaching. Will gestured for him to turn, grasping his shirt hem, and lifting it slightly. Clenching his jaw, he lowered it. "Bridget, point Benjamin to the kitchen please. I need to write this statement. The pair moved to the door, when Will's voice gave them a momentary pause, "Benjamin, is Captain Timmons here in Rochester?"

"Yes, sir. He's staying at the boarding house."

Will gave a nod in reply, and dismissed them. As soon as the door clicked closed, Will gasped for breath. The boy's back was a myriad of black and blue marks, some in the latter stages of healing. Curling his hands into fists, Will cursed the man who saw fit to beat a child, and was genuinely fearful for his sister if this monster was hunting her.

Appalachian Mountains
August, 1863

Emma wiped the sweat from her brow, trying to ignore the

headache rising behind her eyes from the thick moisture in the air. Her stomach did a flip as they walked along the trail. It was about noon when she begged Colin to break for the day, slumping against a tree before he could answer.

"There is a small spring about a mile or so out. I would like to reach it by nightfall." He was studying the map and squinting ahead. "Can you..." He tucked the map into his pack and stopped cold at the sight of her. "Emma, my goodness, what is it?"

Emma smiled weakly, as Colin brought her a canteen. She let the coolness of the water coat her parched throat. "Thank you. I have been feeling a bit queasy these past few days. I was sure it was the heat."

He tenderly cupped her face in his hands. "Emma, I have something very...forward to ask you."

Touching the back of his hand, Emma gazed into his eyes. "Of course."

"Are you with child?"

Her cheeks flushed. "I..."

"Do not feel ashamed, my dear. It was a risk we took by becoming lovers." He covered her face with kisses. "As soon as we can find a preacher, I am marrying you. Our child will not be born out of wedlock."

Emma gazed out at the green mountains and misty white clouds above. "Where would we find one in this place?"

Colin raised her to her feet and embraced his soon-to-be wife. "I do not know, but I am determined in this matter." He caressed her still-flat abdomen. "I could not be more proud or in love with you than I am at this very moment in time, Emma."

She let out a laugh. "What an unconventional pair we are, Doctor McCafferty."

He swung her around, before remembering her delicate state. "Seeing as we may not get out of these mountains before winter, I want us to find a place to stay for the duration. It is a shot in the dark, but I am sure we will succeed."

A massive weight lifted off her shoulders, Emma's steps felt lighter as they continued on their journey. Colin was tender and considerate of her, but to the point where he did not smother his headstrong fiancée. By the time the sun set in an orangey glow over the horizon, they had arrived at their destination by the rippling stream.

Falling to her knees, Emma drank the crystal-clear mountain water, reveling in the sweet coolness of the liquid. She splashed her warm face, and giggled like a child, never realizing how beautiful the simple pleasures in life were before this moment.

"Colin, I would live here, if we could. I fear my family would miss us terribly if we disappeared."

Colin began gathering wood for a fire. "Of that, I am certain."

Emma removed her pack, perching it against a tree. She loosened the collar of her shirt and began preparing some food for their meal. The thought of another evening of hard tack and salt pork made her stomach turn, but the baby needed nutrition. Emma swallowed back the rising bile in her throat, and made quick work of the task at hand.

"Oi there!" A masculine voice broke through their thoughts. Colin moved towards Emma, pulling her behind him. Into the little clearing strode a man and a woman, simply dressed, carrying a few baskets. The man had a scraggly, black beard and matching hair, outlining kind, blue eyes. He was nearly a head taller than Colin. The woman was about the same size as Emma, with wispy, blonde hair and sparkling green eyes.

Colin hesitated before answering. "Hello, can we help you?"

The man spat out a bit of tobacco juice. "Don't worry none, mister. We're not here to turn ya in to anyone." He chuckled deep, his belly jiggling. "But, ya see, nothin' gets past us in these parts. My name's Jim Davis, but everyone calls me Big Jim, and this is my wife, Bessie."

Bessie beamed at Emma. "Hi there!"

"We know that a lot of men come through here lookin' for a way home, but I's told Bess here that you weren't like them. Thought you'd like something other than those army rations. You're welcome to come stay at ours. Ain't nothin' fancy-like, but it's cozy."

Colin wrapped an arm around Emma's waist, drawing her to his side. "That would be very kind of you." His tone must have betrayed some element of worry and slight mistrust.

"Lookie here, I know you wouldn't be in this here mountain range for no good reason. We're not here to judge. Folks keep to themselves, but Bess was raised proper Christian-like and said we should be charitable." Big Jim held out his hand and Colin shook it with a grin.

Together, they gathered up their belongings. Big Jim took hold of Emma's pack and the two women walked along ahead, chatting about everything from dress patterns to cooking. Emma told Bessie about the social outings in Rochester. By the time the four arrived back at their cabin, Emma and Bessie were fast friends. Anticipating the needs of someone who had been traveling the back trails of the mountains, Bessie immediately sent the men to draw water for a bath, filling a copper tub before the fire for Emma.

Colin chuckled at how easily the slight woman commanded her hulk of a husband. Big Jim joked, "She'd pound me over the head with the cast-iron frying pan, sure as anything!"

After the four were fed, Bessie bundled Emma into a spare nightgown, and shuttled the yawning woman off to bed. Big Jim and Colin sat by the fire, discussing the war.

"Too many men dyin' for a needless cause, if you ask me." Big Jim blew a puff of smoke from his cigar towards the ceiling. Colin was not sure where he got it during times of rationing, but he did not question the man.

"I suppose, to some, it seems like that. Have you heard any news about the Army of the Potomac?" Colin was curious as to the whereabouts of their former regiment.

Big Jim eyed him. "I reckon that's where you and the lil' missy there came from?"

Colin reluctantly nodded. "We had...extenuating circumstances."

"Can't say I've heard much. Not since that battle at Gettysburg."

Colin's expression darkened. "Yes, we managed to pick up some news of that before we left into the mountains."

Big Jim leaned back in his chair, the wood creaking slightly. "Well, y'all are welcome to stick around for a bit. I do a bit of lumberjack work and trade some. Could use a spare hand. Y'all don't want to be in the open when winter hits. Couple o' folk'd offer you shelter, but it's rare for us to take in someone from the outside."

"Again, very kind of you. Emma is...with child."

Big Jim whistled and grinned. "I take it y'all are not in the marital way?"

Colin clenched his jaw, and cast his eyes down. "No. We are formally engaged, but I want to make sure our child is born to married parents."

"Now, there's somethin' I can help you with. There's a pastor not far from here. Had some sort of religious vision, and came to live in these mountains. Bet you, sure as anythin', he'd hitch you two! All the same in the eyes of God, I'm told."

Relieved, Colin clapped the man on the shoulder. "I cannot tell you how grateful I am."

"Preacher John usually has some services tomorrow, being Sunday and all. We could take y'all over after breakfast."

Colin felt his concerns over accepting their offer of shelter slipping away. As the evening progressed, he was more at home with Big Jim, having missed the male companionship of the army. They laughed about childhood memories, and shared a bottle of homebrew whiskey. When Bessie returned, both men were snoring in their chairs, tin cups perched precariously in their laps. She shook her head and retired to bed, leaving the men to their torturous sleeping positions.

The sun rose bright on the Sunday morning following Colin and Emma's arrival to the Davis' dwelling. Bessie woke Emma, excitedly retelling the plans she had overheard the previous night. Emma rubbed her eyes in disbelief, as she was hurried from the bed, and to breakfast. Colin and Big Jim were pretty worse for wear, but tried to put on brave faces.

"Bessie darlin' do you have a dress you could loan Emma? I'm sure the preacher will appreciate the effort." Big Jim downed the last dregs of his coffee.

Slapping him on the shoulder lightly, Bessie scoffed as she spooned eggs onto Colin's plate. "You silly man! Don't you think I haven't already thought of that? A wedding! How wonderful! Most excitement I've had in God knows how long!" Bessie quickly hugged Big Jim, and Colin chuckled at the affection between the pair.

Emma sat in awe of the preparations evolving around her. By the time breakfast was finished, Bessie laid out her own wedding dress, a delicately laced white gown. It had been carefully packed in a trunk between folded sheets with lavender sachets. Shooing the men off, Bessie implored Big Jim to help Colin find something suitable.

"Bessie, however did you get something so beautiful? I did not think..." Emma clamped her lips shut, realizing she might have been somewhat rude to her hostess. She flushed with shame.

Bessie patted her hand. "Oh, Emma. Big Jim and I did not always live in these mountains. My papa lived in

Charleston. My Jimmy worked for him and we eloped." She sighed romantically.

Emma ran her fingers over the gown. "You do not mind?"

"Of course not! It would give me great pleasure to see it bring you happiness." Bessie fussed over Emma, who reveled in the feeling of feminine garments on her body once again. A solitary tear slid over her cheek.

Bessie hugged her close. "You will have a lovely celebration at home with your family. I just know it." She held Emma at arm's length, tucking a curl back and placing a wreath of woven flowers on her head. "There. Pretty as any bride there ever was."

Emma took both her hands. "You remind me so much of my sister-in-law, Bridget. She would be fussing over me, just the same." The tears fell anew, and Bessie rocked Emma in her arms.

"Hush now. You're going to marry that handsome man out there and get home. I have faith." Bessie tucked Emma's hand in hers and they departed the cabin, taking the trail not long followed by the men before them.

As Emma and Bessie broke through the clearing, Emma got her first look at the born-again religious man the pair had spoken of so fondly. Preacher John had a long, white beard and snapping, grey eyes. Although his skin was wrinkled, he had a youthful spirit and greeted them heartily, wire spectacles perched on the tip of his nose. Colin's heart caught in his throat, as he viewed the transformation of Emma. Bessie grinned widely at Big Jim, knowing she had accomplished something wonderful.

The breeze rippled the treetops, as the fresh scent of greenery filled the air. It caught the wavy curls of Emma's hair. Colin reached out and took Emma's hand, kissing it. "You are so stunning. I thought at first I was seeing some woodland nymph." He teased her.

Emma blushed. "I had forgotten what wearing a dress felt like. Bessie is so kind to me."

"Shall we commence?" Preacher John positioned himself before the couple, with Big Jim and Bessie acting as witnesses to the union. "We are gathered here today, in this beautiful mountain air to join together Colin McCafferty and Emma Mansfield. I can think of no better backdrop to their union than this peaceful setting."

As the vows were said, Emma only had eyes for Colin. The love between them blossomed to new heights, as the pair were joined as man and wife. Big Jim let out a whoop as Colin swept Emma into a deep kiss. For a moment, the war raging in other parts of the country was forgotten. Mourning of loss drifted into the background, and a celebration of new beginnings took its place.

15

Rochester, New York
September, 1863

The dusky hotel bar was not a place Will wanted to be, on the cool, autumn, afternoon. He slipped away while Bridget and Wade were napping, pressing a kiss to each of their brows. Pride filled his chest at the thought of the two people he held most dear in the world. The mug of ale was cool in his hand, as he swigged the dark brew.

"Second Lieutenant Mansfield. Did not expect to see you in this part of town." Captain Timmons smirked, taking up the stool next to Will without an invitation.

Will placed his glass down, not meeting the eye of the captain. "Ah, yes, but it is exactly where I expected to find you."

The brass buttons on Captain Timmons' uniform reflected the dim lighting of the establishment. He leaned over the splintered counter and ordered an ale for himself. "I take it you got my message?"

"Why else would I be in this Godforsaken place, instead of home with my family?" Will cast a glance around the room. A few men were slumped over tables, many former soldiers like himself. He recognized the hopeless, vacant stare of addiction, numbing their pain and memories with alcohol, and worse.

"You know I am only here to seek information. I know your family is close with Mrs. Elizabeth Hastings, the supposed aunt of one Emmett Hawkins. I believe the boy spent some time at your bedside during your incapacitation?"

Will wiped away the foam from the ale with the back of his hand. "Yes, I had a fondness for the boy. He was from my hometown, after all."

"You realize it is an offense to harbor a deserter from the Union Army." It was more a statement than a question. Will clenched his hand into a fist.

"I served my country and lost a leg in the process, Captain Timmons. How dare you question my loyalty?"

"Easily. You are soft-hearted. I noticed my boy did not return. More charity, Mansfield?"

Will shifted off the stool, taking up his crutches. "I do not see fit to beat young boys who fail at my bidding. Stay away from my family, Timmons. Seek your vendetta elsewhere." Throwing some coins on the counter, Will exited the premises with relief, thankful to be out of the murky atmosphere.

Captain Timmons remained at the bar, his anger simmering. How dare he confront him in such a manner? Mansfield would regret his tone. Ordering a glass and bottle of whiskey, Timmons proceeded to get hopelessly drunk, ire never settling. His aggressions were taken out on an unsuspecting whore. As he slapped her tearing face, Timmons knew he would do much worse to McCafferty and Hawkins when he caught up with them.

The Soldier's Secret

Appalachian Mountains
October, 1863

The foursome fell into an easy routine after the wedding. Big Jim and Bessie were so accommodating, accepting the extra company into their home with joy. Bessie altered a few of her dresses for Emma, much simpler styles than she was used to back in Rochester. Colin trudged off through the woods every morning with Big Jim on trading expeditions. His doctoring skills came into great demand as word spread, in such a short time, of their habitation in the Davis' cabin. The residents of the mountain area were so grateful, lies quickly flew off their tongues if scouting patrols came looking for deserters.

Bessie helped Emma learn the finer points of cooking, the younger girl never having done so in her own home. Bessie giggled as they attempted to bake bread, and Emma's came out looking like a bit of burnt wood. Colin ate some out of good faith, but even he could not manage more than a few bites. Laughter dissolved amongst the group, and Emma tried again, much more successful the second time around. She blossomed in pregnancy, avoiding the sickness usually accompanying the first months. It was a blissful life, with simple pleasures.

One brisk morning, Big Jim returned hastily, but without Colin. Bessie hurried to him, and they spoke in hushed tones. Emma dried her hands on her apron and studied the pair, worried and fearful. Bessie crossed to her and took up her hands. "Emma, something has happened, and we must get you and Colin to safety."

Her brow creased and Emma fearfully glanced over at Big Jim. He gave her a sorrowful nod. "Someone in our circle has betrayed you for money. It's terrible, Em, but we have t' get y'all further north."

"Why would they do that? We have done nothing to anyone." Tears flowed freely. Emma angrily swiped at them, hating the emotions which seemed to take over her body.

Big Jim's large hand rubbed her back. "We have a plan. Bess and I talked about this before, just in case."

"Where is Colin?"

Shaking his head, he declined to answer. "It's best you don't know, until we can get the danger past."

Bessie drew Emma into their bedroom. "You are my sister, understand? Your husband died in the war, and you came to us, pregnant with no help. Your name is Carolyn Smith."

Changing her into a nightgown, Bessie wet Emma's brow to give her the appearance of being ill. They barely managed to get her under the covers in the bed when a pounding on the door shattered the silence of the cabin. Bessie sat on the edge of the bed, clutching Emma's hand, and murmuring reassuring words. They could hear Big Jim in the other room.

"We know there are deserters in the mountains. You know the consequences of your actions." An unknown male voice echoed to their ears.

"I haven't seen anyone." The defiance in Big Jim's voice was evident. Emma was sure if he found out who betrayed them, there would be consequences.

"Coward! You hide in your mountains while good men die!" Bessie yelped as she heard her husband groan and hit the floor.

The soldiers burst into the bedroom. Bessie stood, blocking the bed. The men were from the Union Army, large and imposing.

"What's this? Two little birds protected by one man!" The voice from earlier emitted from a black-bearded man with beady eyes. He leered at Bessie. She raised her chin slightly.

The other one held back his companion. "Come on...no need to think that."

"We could have our fun. Look, one for each of us." Emma shuddered beneath the blankets.

"Vile men! Abusing poor women in their homes! My sister's husband fought for your cause! She has no man now, and is with child! For shame!" Her voice rose up and she jabbed a finger into the chest of the beady-eyed one.

Emma felt for her pistol, tucked beneath the blankets. Her face burned hot under the perusal of the man. The cold metal under her hand provided little comfort if she could not get the gun targeted in time.

"Leave it. There's no one here. 'Sides, no good to take advantage of women whose husbands fought."

Beady-Eyes grabbed Bessie's face. "This one's didn't. He's curled on the floor in the kitchen." His breath stank and she gagged.

The sound of a hammer being drawn back caused both men to spin around, looking for the threat. Emma withdrew the weapon from her hiding spot, and aimed it. "Get out! My husband didn't die to see you abuse my sister!"

Beady-Eyes dropped his hand to his side. "Not worth it for a piece of mountain ass." He shoved Bessie aside and they stalked from the cabin, not before delivering a kick to the prone Big Jim. The cabin door slammed, the sound reverberating in their ears for a few heart-pounding moments. Bessie hurried to her husband's side, Emma close behind still carrying the gun. She fell to her knees, cradling his head in her arms.

"Colin...you have to tell me where he is. Big Jim needs a doctor!"

Bessie nodded. "A few minutes' walk, north from here, is a root cellar. We dug it to keep things, just in case of raids. It's covered by a patch of moss. He's there. Run, Emma, please!" The bruise on Big Jim's temple was growing larger by the moment.

Emma raced to the bedroom, and threw on her dress over the nightgown, pulling on her boots. She crept from the cabin, peering out in the late afternoon sun. The woods were quiet as she held her breath, listening for the sounds of voices, twigs breaking, anything to indicate she was being watched. Luck was on her side as nothing could be seen. Emma made her way to the hidden root cellar and threw open the doors. Colin blinked in the bright light, as Emma hurled herself into his arms.

"You must come quickly!" They carefully picked their way through the woods, back to the Davis' cabin. Bessie was still on the floor with Big Jim. Colin knelt and examined the man.

"We have to get him into the bed. Emma, Bessie, you must grasp his legs. I will take him under the arms." Together, they managed to get him into the bed, although with the three of them lifting, it was no easy task.

"He has a concussion, Bessie. You must watch him carefully." Colin prodded his abdomen, "No broken ribs, thankfully. He will be sore for a few days."

Big Jim moaned low and his eyes fluttered open. Bessie began to sob, delirious with happiness. "Quiet, woman. Feels like I've had the whole Union Army stompin' on my head."

They all laughed, glad to see Big Jim's sense of humor had not been lost, even after the attack on his person.

"You will have to remain in bed for a few days. Watch his breathing while he sleeps, Bessie. He should be out of the woods by tomorrow evening. As for us, I think we should be moving on." Colin's voice hinted at a great reluctance to leave the company of two such good people. The sadness in Emma's eyes mimicked the same feelings.

Bessie hugged them both tightly. "I understand. I wish we could convince you otherwise."

"It would be terrible to put you and Big Jim in such danger, Bessie."

Emma quietly retired to the back bedroom, packing her bag and changing back into her clothing, leaving the dress folded on the bed. Twisting her hair up in a knot, she jabbed a hairpin through it, and tucked her hat over the auburn tresses. Emerging from the room, she did her best to cover up the tears falling, but failed miserably. Bessie and Emma clung to each other for a few moments.

"After this war is over, you have to come to Rochester. Please." Emma implored.

Bessie nodded vigorously, her own tears falling in turn. "We will. We promise."

Big Jim raised a hand and clasped Colin's in his own. "Safe travels. Take some food. Be careful. Not all us folks out here are as kind."

"Find shelter soon. Winter here will kill a man sure as anything." Bessie hustled a few baskets of food into their hands.

"How long do we have?" Colin removed the basket from Emma's arms, and took it himself.

Bessie cast a furtive glance back at Big Jim. "A month, at most. Maybe less."

"Thank you for everything."

"We will meet again. It's in the cards." Big Jim winked and the pair departed the cabin, melancholy descending like a cloud.

Rochester, New York
October, 1863

Will made sure Benjamin did not return to Captain Timmons. He was able to convince his father to give him a job as a stock and errand boy for the shop. Benjamin eagerly took on the role, impressing William with his work ethic. He never questioned his eldest son as to the boy's sudden appearance in the city, although he worried greatly about the clandestine conversations between Bridget and Will. She appeared more frantic as days passed, urging Will to do something. One evening in the parlor, William could take no more.

"What is going on in this household!?"

Rose jumped at her husband's barking voice. "William, dearest, I have no idea what you mean."

William eyed them suspiciously. "Do not assume I am a fool, Rose. Why haven't we heard any news from Emma? I know something must be the matter. This is my house, and I want to know why you all go silent when I walk into a room."

Rose, Will, and Bridget exchanged a worried glance, before Will spoke up. "Father, there has not been any news from Emma because..."

Rose took up the explanation as Will faltered, "Because we do not know exactly where she is."

The strain in the room was palatable. Bridget glanced down at her folded hands, the only sounds coming from the mantel clock ticking. William rose to his feet and exited the parlor, heading through to the back garden area. He paused under a tree and gazed upward at the fading sun, a crisp breeze hitting him in the face. Rose's light footsteps rustled the grass as she approached her distraught spouse. Touching him lightly on the arm, Rose waited for William to speak.

"How long have you known about Emma?" There was a hitch in his voice.

Rose rested her cheek on her husband's arm. "A few months."

William's arms came around her and hugged her close. "Were you concerned about my reaction?"

"In truth, we did not want you to worry. Will came back to us, injured, but alive. Harrison is lost and now, Emma." Rose murmured into his shirt, breathing in the scent of wood packing from the store.

"My darling, I wish you had told me. To bear this burden for such a long time without being able to confide in me must have been very difficult."

Rose gazed up at him with adoration, placing her hand

on his cheek. "It was, but what may be more difficult to comprehend, is what our dear Emma has done."

"Done?" William's brow creased, fearing the reason for their daughter's absence.

"You must understand she did it out of love...for us, and for Will and Harrison."

William tucked her arm through his, and strolled back to the house. "I am not sure I wish to hear more. Is she alive?"

Rose's silence told him everything he needed to know. They returned to the house in a fog, neither wishing to discuss the possible demise of their only daughter.

Appalachian Mountains
Somewhere in Pennsylvania
November, 1863

Emma's teeth chattered, as the sudden breeze ripped through her coat. The travelers were hardly prepared to survive a harsh winter in the mountains without proper shelter. Colin tucked his arm around her, and gave a look around at their surroundings. It had been nearly a month since leaving the Davis' cabin, and they had yet to come across any signs of life. The odds of making it back to Rochester were dangerously low.

Traversing the trails was becoming more difficult as the cold stiffened their limbs. Worse, supplies were running low. Colin was frantic to find some sort of shelter, lest the weather cause damage to Emma or the baby. The tree branches rustled lightly, carrying the sound of singing. The low, gravelly voice rose above the cold. "Makes me feel like my time ain't long..." As they broke the clearing, a man came into sight. He was stooped, wearing a fur-lined coat over a checkered flannel shirt, tan trousers, and work boots. His hat was pulled low over his white hair, a matching beard gracing his face, standing out against his dark skin. He was chopping wood with vigor, stopping every so often to hit a particular key note.

"Well! Is ya gonna stand there gawkin' or come o'er here to says hi to Ol' Tim?" He tipped his hat back, and gave them a grin. He was missing a fair few teeth.

Colin tucked his hand through Emma's and approached.

"Now, ya ain't some fugitive slave hunters? 'Cause I's gots no time for that at my age!" He let out a wheezy laugh, inspecting them through sparkling, brown eyes.

Colin relaxed, smiling. "No, sir. We are just traveling. Slavery was outlawed in these parts back at the beginning of 1863."

"Well, shoot me dead!" He walked closer, evidently bearing a strong limp. "So, what brings ya and yers to my neck of the woods? Been nigh on five years since I've seen nobody!"

Emma raised her head to the sky. "Shelter. Just for the winter months. We have not seen any cabins for miles."

"People 'round 'ere tend to keep to themselves, missy. They no want to be seen unless there's somethin' in it for 'em!" Ol' Tim eyed her distended belly, "Can't see no reason not to let y'all stay wi' me. Don't look like y'all cause me much trouble. Gettin' ol' ya see. Needs me a bit o' help."

Colin displayed visible relief. "We would be happy to help in any way, sir. I would be glad to look at any ailments as well. I am a doctor."

Ol' Tim displayed another toothy grin. "Ya's lucky ya found me. What's your names?"

Emma stepped forward. "I am Emma McCafferty, and this is Doctor Colin McCafferty, my husband." Colin beamed with pride, as she introduced them as man and wife for the first time.

"Oh, yis, I sees. Newlyweds, eh? With that war ragin' in the North and the South, I's figured it would change people." He waved a gloved hand. "Come on in then. Y'alls look chilled to the bone!"

Ol' Tim opened the small cabin door, and the warmth of the fireplace hit Emma. She smiled so broadly, Colin thought her mouth was going to break. It had been some time since they were this warm. The cabin was cozy, sporting a handmade bed in the corner, with a rumpled quilt, sturdy table and chairs, and a chest. There was a rifle hooked over the fireplace. Ol' Tim must have recognized Colin's interest in the firearm.

"Don't you worry none, son. Jes' for huntin' and the like." He hobbled over to a peg by the door and removed his jacket and hat. Heading over to the fire, he swung a kettle of water over the blaze. "Sit! Ya's look dead on yer feet!"

Colin guided Emma to a chair and she gladly allowed him to remove her overcoat, collapsing onto the seat. Ol' Tim gestured to the pegs and Colin hung the garment as well as his own. "What do you do to survive out here, sir?"

"Ah, none a' that sir stuff wi' me. Jes' Ol' Tim'll do me fine. I's hunt, farm a bit when the weather's good and proper. Has me a larder full o' vegetables. More'n 'nough to share." The water began to boil and Ol' Tim brewed some coffee. Handing a tin cup to Emma, she eagerly consumed the warm brew. Colin did likewise, but at a slower pace. He worried about Emma's condition, and knew she should not be out in this wilderness.

"I see's ya love the girlie, Doc. Don't worry none. We'll see her an' the babe through this here winter." He gestured to Emma, whose eyelids were beginning to droop, "Put her in ma bed, don't need it no how."

Colin scooped up his tender burden and lowered her onto the straw mattress, brushing auburn tendrils away from her face. Placing a hand on her gently-rounded belly, Colin bestowed a kiss on her brow and she smiled, drifting off into sleep. He returned to Ol' Tim, joining him at the table for a cup of coffee. The man began putting together the makings of a venison stew. After living off salt pork and hard tack for nearly three months, with the occasional fish, Colin's mouth began to water.

Ol' Tim shook the knife in Colin's direction. "Now, I's gonna be honest with ya so I's expect the same from ya. No lies. How did ya end up in these here mountains?"

Colin commenced telling the tale of their arrival to the Appalachians. He spared little detail in an effort to gain complete trust from their host. By the time he finished, the coffee had been long drunk, and the stew was simmering away on the fire.

Ol' Tim let out a whistle between his teeth. "Ya have come a long way, that's the God's truth. Nearly as far as me." His bones cracked as he stood, hovering over his cooking with a long wooden spoon. Stirring the bubbling mixture sent a new wave of smells into the air. Emma's stomach rumbled and she woke from her slumber, joining the men at the table.

"You, missy, are a brave lady, that's fo' sure." Ol' Tim began to ladle the stew into wooden bowls, placing one in front of each before taking his seat. Without much pomp, the trio swallowed mouthfuls of the nourishing stew.

Emma tried to remember her manners, but months of living off the land made her realize food was more of a necessity than something standing on formality. After draining half her bowl, Emma turned to Ol' Tim. "How did you end up in the mountains? Many people here seem hesitant to help travelers."

Leaning back in his chair, Ol' Tim patted his belly. "Well, see, when I's was a young man, not much older than ya man here, I's worked on a plantation in th' South." His audience captivated, he continued his tale, "Me, I was a hellion, so says the mastah. I's was always runnin'. But, they's catched me and drug me back. Mastah would say, 'Timmy boy! Why do you always run? Don't you know they are just going to drag you back and whip you silly?' And I's say, 'I needs to be free!' He'd laugh, 'Ain't no freedom for your kind, boy. Best just to do your work quietly.' But I's jes' could not listen."

Emma frowned. "Enslaving a human being is so wrong." Her mother's principles were well engrained in her daughter.

Ol' Tim nodded his head slowly and stroked his beard. "I's reckon ya is one o' the few, missy, but I's appreciates the sentiment."

Colin urged him on. "What happened next?"

"Well, there was no way I's was gonna live under the lash o' another man. So's we had this boy who comes to the slave quarters one night. He's all quiet-like an' he says he can run some of us to the north. Freedom."

"The abolitionist movement was in its infancy then. I am surprised there were people fleeing." Emma finished her meal and leaned forward.

Ol' Tim whistled again and chuckled low. "People ain't got no right to hold others. My ma, she came here on a boat from Africa. She say to me, 'My boy, one day, you's is gonna be free!' I's took her words to heart. So I's tells the man to sign me up!" Rubbing the back of his neck, Ol' Tim let out a yawn. "Seems we'll have t' continue another night, missy."

Emma opened her mouth to protest, but Colin silenced her. "We understand."

"Ya can ha' the bed, if ya want." Ol' Tim's bones creaked as he rose again.

Colin shook his head. "The bear skin by the fire will more than suffice, Ol' Tim. We have plenty of blankets."

Bowing his head and smiling, Ol' Tim moved to his bed and fell on the covers, wrapping the quilt over his form. It was not long before his soft snores filled the cabin. Emma removed her boots and exterior clothing, joining Colin under the blankets. He snickered softly and she gave him a defiant stare.

"Sorry, Emma. Still not used to seeing you in red long-johns."

She swatted at him playfully, and sighed as his arms engulfed her. Sleep came quickly to the pair, along with the overwhelming feeling of relief they had a secure place to wait out the winter months. As the wind picked up outside the small cabin, snow flurries flickered through the air, while the trio slept in relative warmth and comfort.

Brandy Station, Virginia
December, 1863

Captain Timmons tapped the neatly folded piece of parchment against his hand. The Army of the Potomac was settling into their winter quarters without much assurance as to their position in the war. The last battle fought between the two forces at Mine Run proved an inconclusive end to the year of conflict. Frustration at the incompetence of the commanding forces made Timmons' blood rise in his gullet. He studied the paper, bemoaning the lack of messenger to deliver such sensitive information.

"Damn Mansfield." Muttering under his breath, Timmons tossed the paper onto his writing desk in disgust. The boy, Benjamin, was no longer in need of his services having established respectable employment in a store. It was inconvenient, but not something which would hinder his goals entirely.

"Bates!" Timmons barked towards the opening to his tent. Private Bates hurried in, saluting and standing at attention. "I need you to take this to the general store owner, and make it snappy."

"What..." Bates bit back his words. The previous months had taught him not to question the motivations of his superior officer, however deplorable he thought them to be.

Timmons rose from behind the writing desk. "Do not think of mentioning this to anyone, you hear me? I'll have no shame in reporting you for murder."

The color rose on the back of Bates' neck. He was waiting for the moment the captain would try blackmail. As long as

Hawkins and Doctor McCafferty got away, Bates knew he had to protect them at all costs. He took the proffered missive, and tucked it into his coat pocket.

"I will deliver this right away, sir." Bates turned to leave, wanting to escape his presence as quickly as possible.

"Oh, and Bates?"

Freezing, as he was about to step through the exit, Bates did not turn around, his disrespect both shaming and empowering. "Yes, sir?"

"Do tell me if you hear anything from your friends, Hawkins and McCafferty, will you?"

The muscles in the back of his neck tensed, fingers curling into a fist. "Yes, *sir*."

"Very good. You are dismissed, Private." Captain Timmons could not help but smile to himself at the discomfort he was causing this man. Pulling out a flask, he imbibed a generous amount of alcohol, reclining back in his chair for a well-earned rest.

Appalachian Mountains
December, 1863

The winds howled viciously around the small cabin, rattling the small-paned windows furiously. Ol' Tim smiled reassuringly at Emma, one of his top teeth missing, "Don't ya fret none, Miss Emma. Th' storm'll soon pass."

Colin stood by the window watching the white flurries whip past. "It certainly is fierce. I hope we brought in enough wood and food to last."

Another pot of thick stew bubbled away over the fire, flames flickering as the cold air spiraled down the chimney, but never faltering. Ol' Tim had taken advantage of Emma's few skills as a cook, and fresh biscuits were rising like fluffy clouds in the small stove he kept, but rarely used. Emma watched them brown slowly, as she thought of dear Bessie.

She wondered if Big Jim had recovered from his injuries, and if they would meet again. Hugging a woolen blanket around her shoulders, she felt the fluttering kicks of the babe growing in her womb. It was a comforting sensation, reassuring her life still existed amongst a world of death.

Colin returned to Emma's side, placing a kiss on her brow and gently caressing her abdomen. The two most important people to him were right by his side, and he would not have it any other way. Ol' Tim smiled at the tenderness between the couple, giving the stew a strong stir with his long wooden spoon.

"I's remember, a young girl from th' plantation."

Colin and Emma immediately gave him their attention. Ol' Tim's stories of slave life were as rare as gold, and only told when he desired to do so.

"Her voice was sure purdy. Sang all day. She worked in th' big house, ya see. Th' master didn't like spoilin' his house slave so's they's was always purdy." His voice betrayed his deep admiration for this woman, yet, a hint of sadness as the lines around his eyes crinkled ever so slightly.

"Go on, please, Ol' Tim. What happened to her?" Emma's soft voice urged him on.

Placing his hands on his worn trousers, Ol' Tim whistled low and leaned back in his chair. "I's decided I's was gonna court her. Went up to th' big house one day and give her th' biggest bunch a flowers I's could find. Well, if she wasn't right pleased. Says t' me, 'Timmy boy, ain't you jes' sweeter than a pot of honey in July!' I's looked down and ask'd her iffin she would like to walk wi' me that night and she's says yes. Well, I's almos' skipped back to mah shack."

Colin threaded his fingers through Emma's, hoping the story would end happily, but somehow knowing it would not.

"Well, we had great times, me and Annabelle. I's wanted to marry her...but th' master...he done sold her off when he saw. Ya lucky, and it fills my heart seein' ya together."

Emma wiped a tear from her eye. "That is so sad though."

"Ah, yeah, it's sad, Miss Emma, but I's knew love. To know love is better than not." Ol' Tim grinned again. For someone whose life was constantly fraught with change and uncertainty, he had learned to cling to the happy memories. He went back to humming and rocking, watching the stew simmer.

Colin knelt by Emma's side. "Have you thought of names?"

"If the baby is a boy, I would like to call him Harrison."

"I agree completely. A great honor to your brother. Go on."

Emma gave his hand a squeeze. "If the baby is a girl, I would like to name her after your mother, but I do not know her name."

Ol' Tim's eyes were closed at this point, but they knew he was listening. It was a small comfort to know someone was interested in their lives.

"My mother's name was Anna. I wish I could have known her. It was hard growing up with a father who barely acknowledged your existence, and blamed you for the death of his only love."

"How could you be to blame?" Emma brought his hand to her lips. "Would you allow her name to live on in our child, should it be a girl?"

Colin's expression lightened. "Of course, my love. Nothing would make me prouder. Come to think of it, I do fancy a girl, with her mother's beauty."

"Sounds mighty nice." Ol' Tim murmured from his chair. "I's suppose we should eat this here stew now, an' some o' Miss Emma's biscuits."

Rising from her chair, Emma set out the tin bowls and cups on the table, pulling the fresh, hot biscuits from the stove. Soon the cabin was filled with the aroma of food, and mouths began to water. The trio dug eagerly into the hearty meal, pausing only to sing the praises of the chefs. Emma and Ol' Tim laughed and joked about how she had burned her first batch, despite following Bessie's instructions to the letter.

As they concluded the meal, the whirling winds came to a stand-still. Colin raised his head upward. "Listen."

A peaceful calm had descended around them. Ol' Tim shuffled to the cabin door and opened it, snow coming up to his waist. "I's reckon we had better push this here snow back jes' a bit."

Colin agreed, pulling on his boots and lacing them tightly. The men pulled on overcoats, tying scarves around their faces and putting on warm gloves. Emma went to the stove and began to boil water in the old kettle, knowing they would need warming up upon their return. Breaking through the wall of fresh powder, Colin edged a path in the direction of the food store. Ol' Tim followed closely behind, stamping down the snow to make a safe path. Emma hurried around the cabin, tidying things away and brushing the snow off the entry.

As predicted, when the men came back, they were more than appreciative of the coffee. Colin hefted half a deer into the cold larder. "That should last us a few more days."

"I's been thinkin'..." Ol' Tim lowered his body into a chair, "I's think y'all should stay 'til that there lil' 'un is born."

Emma passed a cup into his hands. "Are you sure? It is an awful imposition."

"I's don't mind none. No one bothers me. I's can get into town and get some things. People don't care much no how for an ol' black man." He pulled off his gloves and wrapped his fingers around the cup, leaching warmth from the hot liquid inside.

Colin shut the cold larder door and came over to the table. "That is very kind of you. We do have money, so I would like to pay you for the extra supplies."

"T'ain't no worry, Doc. Yer givin' me plenty by the

company. That babe'll need some clothes and such though. I's sure we can get somethin'."

"I am quite sure there is time enough yet. I estimate spring before we have to worry much." Emma put a protective hand over her tender burden. "Now, I do believe it is time to get some rest."

The men were more than happy to oblige, Colin taking Emma to their pallet by the fire. Ol' Tim had strung a curtain across the room with an old quilt for privacy. Snores punctuated the silence of the cabin as the old man found his sleep. Emma curled herself into Colin's arms with a satisfied sigh.

"Content, my love?" He breathed in the fresh scent of her hair, but his answer did not come. He was rewarded with the soft, even breathing of the woman he desired above all. Resting his cheek atop her auburn curls, Colin found the sweet arms of Morpheus.

Rochester, New York
January, 1864

Another Christmas season passed with missing husbands, sons, brothers, and loved ones. The Mansfield family did their best to make it a jovial occasion for young Wade, who delighted in the crinkled paper and fabrics, cooing over wooden toys and a new ball. William had safely hidden away the youngster's presents in the storeroom of his shop for the appointed day. Will bestowed upon his wife simple gifts; a new pair of gloves and stationery. His father did likewise. It was a sparse Christmas, but not without love and laughter.

The days following the holiday were met with visitors from around the town. One brisk morning, crunching through the newly fallen snow, Mrs. Hastings found herself at the Mansfield's door. Adjusting her bonnet, she rapped her knuckles against the wooden frame. As usual, Wade toddled to the door, closely followed by his laughing mother. Her affable mood faded when she spotted the elderly woman on their front porch.

"Mrs. Hastings, do come in out of the cold." A wave of dread permeated Bridget's form.

Entering the house, Mrs. Hastings removed her outer coat and gloves, handing them to a waiting maid. “Thank you kindly, my dear. My, my! How young Wade has grown!” She smiled warmly to the sturdy toddler.

Bridget scooped up her son, and gestured to the parlor. “Shall we sit? Mother Rose is working on some needlepoint.”

“Thank you kindly, my dear. Some tea would not go amiss either.” Although bold, something seemed particularly off about Mrs. Hastings’ nature. Bridget politely asked the maid for some tea to be brought to the parlor, before following her in.

Rose set her needlepoint aside, a frosty expression engulfing her features. “Mrs. Hastings. We were not expecting visitors today.”

Bridget warily settled Wade on the floor next to the iron fire grate with his wooden animals. She lowered herself next to her son, smoothing her skirts and watching the interaction.

Mrs. Hastings gracefully brushed a kiss on Rose’s cheek and sat. “It could not be helped. I have some rather distressing news.”

Rose stiffened, lowering herself back into her spot, hands clenched in her lap. “I do hope it is nothing serious.”

Mrs. Hastings sighed deeply. “Let’s get tensions out of the way, shall we? As I am sure Bridget has informed you of my role as Emma’s accomplice, there is no point letting it hang over our heads. I am well aware she is missing, and her assumed persona listed as a deserter by the Union Army. There is no point dwelling on this fact.”

“Who, in their right mind, would suggest a girl go off to fight in a war?” Rose’s tone was level. Only Bridget knew her mother-in-law was seeing red.

“Emma’s reasoning was she knew neither you, nor Mr. Mansfield, would hear about Harrison, if something had happened to him. It is not often, if at all, people are told these things when their child goes off to fight for the opposing side of a war."

"What made Emma believe she could uncover such information?"

Mrs. Hastings accepted a cup of tea from the maid. "Hope, I suppose. How could I say no? I did warn her of the possible dangers, but she was determined. In fact, she came to me for help."

Bridget gazed up at Rose. "It does sound so much like something our Emma would do. Shouldn't we focus on trying to find out what has happened to her now?"

"Well put, my dear. This is the exact reason I have come. I have had a rather disturbing visit from a man who claims to have known Emmett Hawkins."

"How very strange. So have we." Bridget cast a worried look to Rose.

"Was it an officer? He was quite a horrid looking man, with bushy red hair and bloodshot eyes."

Rose shook her head. "No, I believe ours was a young boy, badly beaten Will tells us. He is working with William at the store, at our insistence, of course. The boy was quite frightened by his whole ordeal."

Mrs. Hastings blew lightly on her tea, before taking a small sip. "I feel this is no coincidence."

Will called out through the house and was answered by Bridget, directing him to the parlor. Wade toddled over to greet his father and was rewarded with a big hug and kiss. Realizing they had guests, Will inclined his head politely. "Mrs. Hastings."

"Hello Will. You are looking quite well." She placed the cup down on a small end table.

"Well under the circumstances." Will glanced between his mother and the elderly visitor, then to Bridget. "May I ask to what do we owe the privilege?"

Rose tapped the seat next to her and Will shifted over to join her. "We were discussing how it seems we have both had an unexpected visitor in the recent months."

"Young Benjamin is doing very well at the store. I have just been to help Father with some accounts. He is thriving, and has put weight on." Will made himself comfortable as much as his leg would allow.

"Were you not visited by an officer, Will? Perhaps one with red hair and a mean temperament?" Mrs. Hastings adjusted the ribbon of her bonnet.

His hand clenched into a fist. "I had the unfortunate pleasure of meeting such a man in an undesirable location in town."

Rose and Bridget were in shock. "You never told us of this encounter, Will." His wife attempted to occupy Wade further, while asking the question.

"I did not see a need to worry you, sweetheart. I do know the gentleman," he scoffed at the word, "in question. A man by the name of Captain Louis Timmons. We served together in the Army of the Potomac, prior to my injury. I warned him away from Benjamin and the family. He was not pleased."

"Did you mention this to your father?"

Will shook his head. "Of course not. I did not think Father would approve of my presence in this location. Judging by recent news, Timmons is far away in Virginia, at the winter quarters."

Mrs. Hastings sighed. "He was very adamant in finding the whereabouts of my nephew...rather...Emma."

"I honestly cannot think of a reason why Emma would be a target for Timmons, except by sheer coincidence. Timmons was not exactly the easiest of men to get along with."

Bridget piped up, "Should we be concerned about this man?"

Will rubbed his leg, eager to stand and pace the room, but knowing it was nigh impossible for him to perform such a task. "There is a possibility, but nothing can be done until the end of the war and we find out if Emma is alive." He regretted the words as soon as they fell from his lips.

Reaching over, Will took his mother's hand in his and gave it a reassuring squeeze.

Rose's voice shook. "It is a possible inevitability we must face."

"If the good doctor is with our Emma, I doubt he would let any danger befall her, Mother Rose."

"I can only hope. In the meantime, we must keep a sharp eye out for this Captain Timmons. He may decide to pay us another visit." Rose managed a weak smile. "We must send all our thoughts to Emma. Who knows what kind of danger she might be in now."

Battle of the Wilderness
Orange County, Pennsylvania
May, 1864

"Move that cannon into place now!" Captain Timmons roared over the deafening racket of bullets and artillery fire whizzing around them. He mentally begrudged his position in this campaign. Lieutenant General Ulysses S. Grant had taken command of all the Union forces, leaving the Army of the Potomac under the command of Major General Meade. They had cobbled together a strategy, dubbed the Overland Campaign, and their forces were now headlong into the first confrontation with the Confederate forces. The goal was to draw Lee out of his fortifications at Mine Run, and force a battle to ensue.

"Sir, we need more powder!" A boy, probably no older than fifteen, raced up to the captain. He was promptly rewarded with a cuff to the back of the head.

"Then get it! No use telling me!" Captain Timmons held onto his hat, as a shell crashed nearby, sending dirt and debris up into the air.

"Sir! We're being asked to withdraw to the courthouse!" Private Bates ducked and weaved to get to Captain

Timmons' side.

"What?! Damnation!" He gave the order and the artillery regiment began to withdraw. Later in the evening, when Captain Timmons was alone in his tent, he imbibed a generous amount of alcohol, passing out on his cot, trying to block out the moans and cries of the wounded. The voices still haunted his nightmares, as did two certain people, who were no longer subject to this madness.

"Sir?" A voice invaded his stupor.

Timmons leaned up on his elbows. "What is it?"

Bates entered the tent. "I thought you should know, there was a message for you." He handed over the worn missive, saluted, and left quickly.

Groaning at his throbbing headache, Timmons sat on the edge of his cot and gulped down water, although it did little to ease his pain. He squinted at the scrunched script on the paper, slowly processing the message. Finally, his connections had proved useful. There had been several raids on cabins in the mountains, where suspected deserters were hiding. A man fitting Captain McCafferty's description had been seen with a young woman. Before anyone could apprehend the pair, they were gone, further north, into the wilderness.

"So," Timmons mused to himself, "McCafferty has abandoned Hawkins. Doesn't seem like something he would do, but oh well." He lit a match and watched the paper burn, the edges blackening, before being consumed entirely by the flame. Withdrawing his own stationery, Timmons sketched a crude drawing of the Union position and planned advance on the Confederate troops.

Folding the paper, he tucked it into his breast pocket. The information would prove crucial in getting him another hefty payment. Maybe after the war, he could retire to California, and live out his days in saloons and whore houses. No one would ask questions. A smile slowly formed on his face. Yes, he would turn in his last report to his superiors, make sure McCafferty saw the noose, and slip into anonymity.

Appalachian Mountains
May, 1864

With the summer months creeping up on them, Colin and Emma hardly noticed the passing time. Their life was very simple with Ol' Tim. The men made sure fresh meat was always available, and Emma tended the simple herb and vegetable garden around the back of the house. Her belly grew and Colin often worried she was working too hard. Brushing him off, Emma reassured him the baby was growing well and kicking constantly. Colin studiously listened for the heartbeat each evening, the sound giving him much comfort. It was a blissful time for all, knowing a new life would be in their midst any week now.

One afternoon, Ol' Tim returned from a supply run, and seemed a bit more antsy than usual. Emma helped him unload the dry goods and remarked on the change in his demeanor.

"I's fine, Miss Emma. Some o' them Union boys were pokin' around, askin' questions. I's jes' a bit nervous. Not sayin' anythin' will happen, but I's suspect we should get stuff ready jes' in case."

Emma relayed the news to Colin when he returned with two rabbits for supper. Quickly agreeing, Colin and Ol' Tim packed away most of their belongings and dry food in one of the trees some distance from the cabin. Anxiety rippled through the cabin. With the winter months at an end, patrols would be resuming for deserters. The evening meal sat uneasily in Emma's stomach. Her lower back ached most of the day, but she attributed it to her work in the garden.

Colin stopped cold and held up a hand. The sound of dogs could be heard in the distance. He cast Emma a worried glance. "We should retire to the woods." Emma nodded without argument. She quickly added layers of clothing to her body and pulled a felt hat low on her head, tucking her hair inside.

Ol' Tim shook Colin's hand and gave Emma a warm hug. "Jes' be careful, ya hear? I's sure they'll pass soon and y'all can come back." He ushered them out the door.

The light was low, but they were still able to see as they made their way through the familiar groves of trees. Reaching the location of their supplies, Colin deftly lowered the bundles and gathered them on his back, handing Emma some lighter ones to carry in her bag. She raised a hand to her mouth and stared at Colin in horror, "The gown I was sewing for the baby...I left it on the table!"

Colin grimaced and pulled her tightly into his arms. "It's too late to go back." Lifting his head, he could hear the barking of bloodhounds was getting closer. Emma swallowed her tears and nodded. "We must hurry." Quickly kissing her, he took her hand and they disappeared into the undergrowth.

They made a small camp, not lighting any fire. Colin sat guard while Emma got some rest. Two shots rang out and Colin's heart dropped to his knees. Leaving a loaded pistol at Emma's side, Colin crept back through the forest to the cabin. The door was flung open and a figure lay in the middle of the dirt outside the cabin. Waiting a few agonizing moments, Colin made sure they were alone before hurrying to the side of the man. Turning him over, he shook his head.

"Colin son, ya shouldna be here." Ol' Tim sputtered violently, as blood splattered from his mouth.

"Hush." Colin pressed a cloth to his mouth and inspected the wound; two bullet shots to the left side. Ol' Tim's lungs would be filling with blood.

"I's dyin' I's know that. Ya must get her home. And the baby." He choked again. "Y'all has made this ol' man's life good. Don't you worry none. Git, now!" Ol' Tim's body heaved and the life slipped from him.

Colin lowered his body to the ground and closed his eyes. Rising to his feet, he went to the cabin and looked inside. The contents had been ransacked. In the middle of the floor was the half-finished gown, torn in two. Colin clenched his jaw and wiped back a tear with his hand. Emma would never forgive herself if she knew. Colin swore an oath never to tell her the truth, if only just to protect her from the misery.

On his walk back to their small camp, he regretted not sending Emma home on the first train possible. This journey was turning into a nightmare. As he entered the clearing, Emma was struggling to sit up. Her face was deathly pale in the moonlight. Rushing to her side, Colin gathered her into his arms.

"Colin...I think...oh no!" She clutched her abdomen and moaned.

"There is time yet. We have to get you indoors. I am sure there is something around here."

Emma winced as Colin gathered their belongings and helped her to her feet. "We cannot go back, can we?"

Shaking his head, he guided her along one of the trails. "No."

"You shouldn't be out on these trails at night, you know." A voice behind them had Colin reaching for his pistol. They turned and saw a hunched old woman with a panting hound dog by her side. "Follow me." She limped past them, using a polished stick to aid her walk.

Emma let out a small whimper, as Colin hesitated.

"Do you want that baby born in the dirt? Follow me!" The order was firm. Colin had little choice at this point. He aided Emma along the path to a caravan in a clearing. The hag gestured with her stick, "Inside. I have some herbs for the pain. Don't worry. I know what they did to Ol' Tim. He was my friend. Foolish to help deserters, mind, but he was lonely." She turned her back, and stirred up the fire.

Not in a position to question, Colin entered the sweet-smelling wagon and unwrapped Emma from her coat, removing her clothing and settling her between the sheets. He remained by her side as contractions tightened her womb in preparation for the birth of their child. The crone brought him fresh linens and a bowl of hot water, leaving them in peace.

The sun was rising the next morning as Emma pushed forth the babe into the world. Exhausted, Colin and Emma beheld their newborn child, a girl, with silent awe. The happiness of the occasion was punctuated with painful memories of Ol' Tim, and how excited he was at the thought of having a baby in his home. Tucking mother and child into the bed, Colin cleaned up and exited the caravan. The old woman handed him a plate of beans and salt pork, as well as a cup of fresh coffee.

"Thank you." Black circles ringed his eyes as he dug into the meager meal.

Waving her gnarled hand in the air dismissively, she sat beside him. "Think nothing of it. Don't much care for what those soldiers are doing here. Although, I 'spect you've been a part of the war."

Colin swallowed before answering her, setting his spoon down. "We both were." Exhaustion took away any censor he might have had.

"I see. Your young wife there must have disguised herself pretty well. Lookie here, get her home and get yourself turned in. Much better than anything those boys will do if they find you. Let her heal and be on your way."

In full agreement, Colin nodded his head and finished his food, pondering the easiest way to accomplish this feat.

Rochester, New York
July, 1864

Two figures cloaked in black rode down the silent streets. A soft cry broke the silence, but was soon quieted by a woman's voice. The pair guided the horses down a familiar road, where one helped the other dismount. They creaked open the long-locked door of Doctor McCafferty's office and disappeared inside, firmly setting the latch. Only then did they feel safe enough to remove their outer coverings. Emma quickly settled the baby, bringing her to feed at her breast. Finally content with the nourishment, Anna swiftly dropped off to sleep.

Colin collapsed into his favorite chair, dusty from his long departure, but no less comfortable. Everything was as he left it, thankfully. He had asked Emma's family to make sure his office remained intact, and they did not fail him. The familiar surroundings were an immediate comfort to both. As much as they wanted to see family and friends, it was better to wait until morning.

The final months of the journey had been arduous. Colin had managed to trade for some horses for the final leg, mocking injury with his concealed face. More than once, they found themselves running from bounty hunters seeking deserters, or Union soldiers on patrol. Coming directly into Rochester was a risk, but one that had to be taken.

"Colin?" Emma's soft voice invaded his thoughts.

His head was back on the chair, eyes closed. "Mmm? Yes, love?"

"We need to think of what to do next." She rocked and hummed to their baby girl.

Colin rubbed his face with a groan. "Yes, I know."

"They will take you to prison, or worse, back to the front." Her brow creased in concern and tears began to flow.

"If only there were a way to implicate Timmons. We could show he drove us from the army. Perhaps my sentence would be lenient then, maybe confined to work at one of the hospitals here in New York."

"I have often tried to think why he developed such a dislike towards me."

Colin leaned forward, forearms resting on his thighs. "Can you think of anything which might have set him off?"

Emma closed her eyes and shook her head. "Nothing. I am so sorry."

"It's alright, my darling love. Let's get some rest. In the morning, we can consider the possibilities." Colin guided her up the wooden stairs to the living area he kept above the office. It was neat as a pin, again left as it was when he departed. Drawing down the blankets and sheets, he helped Emma remove her boots and outer garments. They settled on the bed, Emma's body curled around a sleeping Anna, and Colin at her back. For the first time in many years, sleep came quickly, and without fear.

The Soldier's Secret

Battle of the Crater
Petersburg, Virginia
July, 1864

"Lay the charges." Timmons whispered urgently to several privates under his command. The stifling climate of the mine was closing in on him, and he wanted nothing more than to breathe fresh air. The method of ventilation was clever, and hid their positioning from the Confederates, but it did not make the air any less stagnant. The mine shaft had been slowly dug over the duration of nearly a month, until they were square under the Confederate lines. The plan was to blow the whole thing, devastating the opposing forces and leaving the Army of the Potomac with a clear opening to attack and drive them back.

"Pack it in tight, boys." The 320 kegs, nearly eight thousand pounds, of gunpowder were handed down in a chain and stacked through the shaft of the mine. The men packed an eleven-foot-thick wall of dirt around the mouth of the mine to prevent the charges from blowing out the entrance.

Timmons wiped dirt from his brow. "Let's get the hell out of here, boys." He led the men out of the shaft back to the trenches dug behind the lines. They waited for the order to blow the mine. At 4:44am, the order came. The charges were lit.

The deafening explosion rocked the battlefield. Men, cannon, dirt clods, and small-arms flew violently up into the air. The screams echoed in Timmons' ears, and he pulled his hip flask out for another drink.

A charge was ordered and chaos ensued. Men were sent over the wall of the trench into a virtual slaughterhouse. Timmons shirked back against the trench wall, his heart pounding. The alcohol did nothing to blank out the howls of dying men. He began to quake, as men were sent to die. He watched Bates mount the trench and charge with his compatriots. It was the last time he ever saw the man. Timmons was alone to face his fate, and he decided to run.

Joining the retreating Union forces, Timmons kept his head low and raced away from the bloody battlefield. At the end of the day, the Union had failed miserably in what was meant to be a great offensive maneuver. Their forces lost nearly four thousand men, compared to the meager loss of only twelve hundred by the Confederates, including those blasted to bits by the mine explosion.

Scrambling back to his tent, Timmons consumed the last of his alcohol. The cries would not cease, and he pounded his head ruthlessly until a young private heard the noise and stopped him. Blood poured from a gash at the base of his skull, going unheeded by the captain. The man was so fearful of Timmons he ran to his nearest superior, and reported the disturbing scene. The officer had Timmons removed on grounds of medical reasons. He was to be transported back home for treatment for a head wound. When asked where he lived, the only words Timmons could mutter were, "Rochester."

Rochester, New York
August, 1864

Emma and Colin rose on the first of August feeling refreshed, before the dark cloud rolled over them. They used the very last of their food supplies to have a small breakfast, before Emma heated some water to bathe. The copper tub in the room had not gone unnoticed and she was desperate for a bath. Stripping her clothes, Emma took Anna into the tub as well, cleaning her quickly before handing her off to Colin for fresh clothes and a clean, cloth diaper.

Emma gleefully washed days of dirt off her skin and hair. When she emerged from the tub, her skin was pale and glistening. Colin smiled warmly at her, admiring the womanly figure.

"You are more beautiful in this moment than I could ever imagine. I wish I had the opportunity to write you more letters." Colin chuckled and bounced Anna on his knee, rewarded with a happy gurgle from his daughter.

Stopping cold, Emma blinked a few times. "Colin...I know what to do. We must see my parents now." She quickly donned her clothing, and urged Colin to wash before they left.

"What if someone sees us?"

Emma shook her head. "It will not matter now." She kissed him briskly.

Grabbing her hand, Colin pulled her back. "I have something for you. I was going to wait until we could properly renew our vows in a church, but now seems a better time than any." He took her left hand and placed an intricate gold band on her ring finger. "You are truly mine before God, and the rest of the world." He sealed his declaration with another kiss, sending trembles through Emma's body.

"If you keep kissing me like that, we will never make it out of here." Emma caressed his face, "Thank you, my love. I shall treasure it always."

With everything gathered, Emma and Colin set forth to the Mansfield residence on horseback, Baby Anna cradled in her mother's arms. The yelp emitted by the maid upon seeing Emma at the door drew the entire family from the dining room, where they were having their own breakfast. William immediately ushered the small family into the house as to avoid a scene on the streets.

Many hugs were exchanged between the family members, and quite a few tears shed. Rose cooed over her newest grandchild, while Wade looked on in wonderment at these new people who caused such a great fuss. Emma quickly handed Anna off to Rose, and urged her and Bridget to take the children into the parlor.

"Father, there will be time for admonishments later. I

must speak with you and Will urgently." William nodded and guided the four adults into his study. Colin spoke quietly with Will for a few moments, enquiring as to the healing of his injury and was assured Will was in good health. All found a place to sit and Emma began her tale.

"When I was under the guise of Emmett Hawkins, I seemed to cause the wrath of a captain in my unit. It wasn't until this morning I realized what I may have done." She turned and met Colin's gaze, "I believe Captain Timmons is a spy for the Confederacy."

William held up a hand. "One moment, is this man the same one who sent young Benjamin to question us?" He directed his query to Will, who responded with a solemn nod.

"You mean, you are aware of this man?"

"Yes, he sent a boy to question us, as to the whereabouts of Emmett Hawkins. We decided this boy would be better off with us than at the mercy of a man like Timmons. I warned him away from our family. This is pretty damning information, Em." Will rubbed his absent leg, haunted by phantom pains.

Colin leaned forward. "What makes you think Timmons is a spy?"

"Something that happened the first time I ever encountered him. I did not think anything of it until now when I was trying to find a reason for his ire. You see, he dropped a bit of paper with a map on it. There were very specific battle strategies on it, more so than a captain would have access to."

William rubbed his forehead. "That paper would be long gone by now. It would be his word against yours."

"Question the boy." Will's voice caused his father to look up, "He's sure to know something if he worked for Timmons. If we can formulate some damning evidence as to why Colin and Emma had to flee, Colin might be spared a prison term."

"Of course. He should be eating in the kitchens, waiting

to go to the store."

Will rose, placing the crutches under his arms. "I'll fetch him." He waved off Emma's steadying hand, "No offense, Em, but I've been coping with this for nearly two years. I can manage."

With Will out of the room, William took the opportunity to question Emma and Colin as to their experiences during the journey home. He was more than pleased to find out they were wed before the birth of Anna. Colin chose to reveal to William about the death of Harrison, and their suspicions about Timmons' role in the affair. It did not surprise him, judging on the character analysis of the wayward captain.

Will returned, Benjamin close on his heels. He twisted his hat in his hands, very nervous about the room full of adults before him.

Emma gave him a smile, hoping to ease his discomfort. "Hello, Benjamin. I am Emma McCafferty. We were wondering if we could ask you some questions about Captain Timmons."

Benjamin flew back against the wall, clambering for the door. Will placed a steadying hand on the boy's shoulder. "Hold on now. Emma is my sister. She fought...she fought as a man in the Army of the Potomac."

Curious, Benjamin ceased his frantic behavior and studied the slight woman in the room. "How do you know that man?"

"He commanded my division and murdered my, our brother." She gestured to herself and Will, whose face went pale before he sat. Emma put a hand on her eldest brother's shoulder, "I'm so sorry, Will."

The youth sighed. "I'm sorry, miss. Yes, he took me and said I had to do what he said or my family would suffer. It wasn't until Mr. Mansfield here said it wasn't true, miss. He had me deliver notes to people in towns we passed through."

"Do you know what those notes said? Please, it's very important."

Benjamin shook his head. “No, miss, but I know the names of all the people he had me send them to. Would that help?”

“It very well might.” Emma reassured him.

William stood quickly. “I suggest Colin get upstairs and stay out of sight for the time being, until we can sort this all out with the local authorities. Benjamin, come with me. I will take care of this.” He was on good terms with many of the military authorities in the city. Perhaps his acquaintances would come in handy. As they all exited the study, William stopped his daughter at the door. “Emma, did Harrison…” His voice snagged, and he coughed to cover up his weakness.

Emma wrapped her arms around her father. “Harrison died instantly, Father. He did not suffer. We buried him in the woods outside West Virginia.”

In a rare moment, Emma felt her father begin to sob. He regretted the sudden parting of his youngest boy and wished they could have made peace. Emma let go of her own sadness, properly mourning the loss of her brother. “We said words around his grave, Father. Perhaps, I can read them to you later.”

Taking a cleansing breath, William held his daughter at arm’s length. “Emma, my sweet girl, nothing would please me more.”

De Camp General Hospital
Fort Slocum, New York
September, 1864

“He truly is in a bad state of mind. He keeps muttering about revenge.” The elderly nurse shook her head, as she gave the resident doctor a report of the captain’s prognosis. He had been brought in with special orders to keep him until his head injury mended. Bandages swathed the base of his head, coming around to rest on his forehead.

"We must make him comfortable for the time being."

A messenger panted as he arrived into the room. "'Pologies, Sir, but this here just came for you!"

The doctor opened the hastily penned note and frowned deeply. Laying her hand on his arm, the nurse studied the missive held out for her perusal. She clasped her breast and gasped.

"We must make him comfortable, and no mention of this. It may hinder his recovery greatly. Despite his crimes, we must treat him as any normal patient."

"He will hang for it, I am quite sure!" The nurse clicked her tongue, and shook her head in bewilderment. The pair exited the ward.

Opening one eye, Timmons replayed the words in his head. *Hanged! No! Damnation! Who could have revealed me? Hawkins! That wily brat I lost to the Mansfields! No, I will not hang, but they will die. No witnesses means no proof.* He lay back in his bed and plotted his escape from the hospital. His bag was still under his bed, with more than enough money to get him from Fort Slocum to Rochester. *I'll play the part of a wounded soldier coming home. That will get me more than enough sympathy.*

19

Rochester, New York
September, 1864

The house was quiet as William returned from his meeting with the Union officials. Benjamin immediately retreated into the kitchens for some lunch, as his companion moved to the parlor. Inside, he found his wife and daughter, playing with the children. Emma gazed up expectantly at her father.

"They listened to the entire story, and would like to speak to you tomorrow, Emma. It is no crime what you have done, but they have yet to decide what to do with Colin. I was vague about his return date so the family will not be implicated in harboring a deserter." William collapsed next to his wife, the weight of the world lifted off his shoulders.

Rose took his hand. "Emma told me about Harrison." She wiped away a lingering tear with her handkerchief.

"Oh, my sweet Rose, I am sorry you have had to bear this burden." William tenderly placed an arm around his wife.

"It's alright. Perhaps we could try to pay a visit to his grave...when this mayhem is over?"

"Of course. Now, where's my Anna-bear?" Emma held out the baby girl to her grandfather, who scooped her up into his arms. It was a great blessing to William to have two such beautiful grandchildren to dote upon.

Emma left the happy scene to report the news to Colin. She found him pacing restlessly in her old bedroom, converted for the comfort of the couple and the baby. He stopped suddenly when she entered the room.

"Please tell me you have some good news?"

Emma nodded and went into his arms. "Father says I will not be charged with any crime. Emmett Hawkins has been discharged from the Union Army, with no further action pending. As for yourself, they have yet to decide. Father bought us a few days. They want to speak with me tomorrow." She rested her head against his broad chest.

He rubbed her back rhythmically. "Honesty is the best way to go. Do not try to falsify anything on my account. If I must face a prison sentence, that is how it must be."

"I hope it does not come to such a drastic end. You are a good doctor and loyal to your country. I will make them see."

The subsequent morning, Emma joined her father in the carriage for the short ride to the Union Army headquarters. Tucked in her small drawstring bag were the papers confirming her enlistment in the army, along with a picture taken at the same time. The resemblance between "Emmett Hawkins" and "Emma Mansfield" was undeniable.

The dark red calico dress swayed with each step Emma took, as her father escorted her to the appointed meeting place. The room was cozy, and three officers sat at a long table opposite a single chair. There was a clerk in the corner poised with pen and paper to record the proceedings.

"Miss Mansfield, please be seated." The tallest officer stood and Emma quickly discerned his rank of Lieutenant Colonel.

Adjusting her skirts, Emma primly corrected him. "I am Mrs. Emma McCafferty now."

William sat by the clerk, watching his daughter with a mix of pride and fear.

"I am Lieutenant Colonel Hatting." He resumed his seat and smoothed his uniform coat. "Mrs. McCafferty, judging by the account given by your father, am I correct in stating you enlisted in the Union Army, as one Emmett Hawkins?"

"That is correct, sir." Her back was ramrod straight.

"What were your reasons for doing something so reckless?"

Emma bristled at his quick judgment of her character. "I was seeking information as to the whereabouts of my two brothers, William and Harrison Mansfield."

"And we have been told your youngest brother, Harrison Mansfield, was fighting for the Confederacy?"

Emma replied with a mere nod before continuing. "He was coincidentally captured while scouting my unit's position, sir."

The pen of the clerk scratched the paper, as the panel considered their next question. "Mrs. McCafferty, who did you serve under while in the Union Army?"

"My regimental commander was Captain Louis Timmons." The bile rose in the back of her throat at having to mention the name and she coughed lightly.

"Were you a witness to the execution of Harrison Mansfield by Captain Timmons?"

The question hit her hard and Emma forced back tears. "I was outside the cabin when Captain Timmons emerged, alone, holding a pistol."

"While we are sorry for his loss, it is not an offense for him to have executed a fleeing spy."

Emma lowered her eyes. "Your pardon, but my brother was badly injured. There was no way he was a threat to anyone."

Her statement was ignored. "May we see your enlistment documents?" Emma withdrew them from the bag, and passed them to the clerk who handed the papers to the lieutenant colonel. "Remove your hat, please."

Emma did so. Her auburn hair was coiled around her

head in a fashionable up-do, but there was no mistaking her facial features. One of the other officers scribbled on the paper issuing a discharge on the grounds of sexual incompatibility.

"We would like to ask about the accusations made towards Captain Timmons."

Emma folded the papers back into her bag. "I am afraid I only have little to add. I returned a letter to him that appeared to be clear drawings of the Army of the Potomac's position on the Rappahannock River. The letter was addressed and ready to be posted or delivered. I am not sure."

A few more notations were made and Lieutenant Colonel Hatting fixed his gaze on Emma. "I understand your husband, Captain Colin McCafferty, fled with you?"

"He was not my husband at the time, but we were promised. We married along the way back to Rochester. We have a daughter, sir."

The lieutenant colonel had seen many deserters come through his office, and he knew a prison term was a death sentence for some. There was a shortage of doctors at the front and back in the hospitals. It would be a shame to lose one who was doing only what he thought was honorable. The woman before him was poised and elegant. He had a hard time imagining her fighting alongside men, while artillery shells rained down. To reward her bravery and gumption with the loss of her spouse seemed unduly harsh. They had brought evidence of a suspected spy into their midst.

"Mrs. McCafferty, your husband must report here tomorrow morning for reassignment. He will be demoted to first lieutenant, and told to report to De Camp General Hospital. I have reports from his superiors here and, by all accounts, he is a competent doctor. It would do no good to see him lost in a prison."

Emma's face broke out in a beaming grin. The lieutenant colonel felt himself blushing in her presence. "Thank you, sir."

As the interview was adjourning, a private rushed into the room, a telegram thrust before him. "Apologies, sir, but they said it's urgent!"

William stood and moved to his daughter's side. "I hope it is nothing distressing."

Lieutenant Colonel Hatting frowned. "Best get your daughter home, Mr. Mansfield. Captain Timmons broke himself out of De Camp General Hospital last night."

Millie's screams from the kitchen brought Mrs. Hastings to full attention in her small parlor. The man who burst through the door had the look of a complete madman. His head bandages had not been changed in several days, and were saturated with dried blood. Raising her head, she recognized the man immediately.

"Captain Timmons. This is an unexpected surprise." Maintaining her calm and dignity would be key.

A Colt Pocket came into view. "Where is Emmett Hawkins?"

"I have no idea what you mean. My nephew is missing." The shot fired off into her China cabinet elicited a yelp from the elderly woman, as the glass shattered.

"I will not ask again! I know he's back here! I know!" Timmons put a hand to his head with a groan, pain ripping through his skull.

Gesturing to a seat, Mrs. Hastings tried to calm the man. "Sit and rest. You must be in a lot of pain."

"Enough stalling!" Timmons leveled the gun with her head. "Take me to Emmett Hawkins!"

Mrs. Hastings raised her hands, submissively. "I am an old woman. I have lived my life well enough."

The deafening click of the hammer being drawn back caused Mrs. Hastings' heart to nearly stop beating in her chest. The slamming of the back door made Timmons lose focus, and Mrs. Hastings pushed past him. He stumbled over his feet and fell to the floor, hastily aiming at the fleeing woman. He cursed loudly, pushing himself upright and stalking to the kitchen. The door wavered in the breeze. Exiting the house, he spotted the black servant running down the street. Lowering the hammer back into position gently, Timmons pursued her.

Millie made it to the Mansfield residence in record time. She feared for the safety of her mistress, but knew she had to warn the family of the madman. As soon as she heard the name, Millie was planning her flight. She flung open the front door, shouting for help. Her cries were silenced by a sharp blow to the head by Timmons' pistol as he slammed the door shut, having reached the house almost instantly after her.

The remaining members of the family, including the children, were at the mercy of a man with a maniacal agenda and bound by revenge. Colin heard the commotion downstairs and reached for his handgun, positioning himself at the top of the stairs. Emma and her father unknowingly entered the home at the beginning of the confrontation. All she could hear were the demands Emmett Hawkins be brought out.

The children wailed in the parlor. Colin whistled and Emma glanced upward. She motioned for her father to move to the study swiftly. He kept a rifle in there for emergencies. As much as William wanted to rescue his wife and grandchildren, he put his trust in Emma. Raising her hands, Colin watched helplessly as his wife entered the parlor.

Timmons whirled around at the newcomer and aimed his handgun. Rose smothered a scream, Anna in her arms. Bridget clutched to her side. Will was frozen on the settee, unable to move as his crutches had been brutally thrown aside, holding Wade on his lap and doing his best to shield the toddler from harm. Rage burned in his eyes.

"Who are you?" Captain Timmons grabbed Emma's arm

in a brutal vice.

Emma clenched her teeth. "Let me go."

Timmons shook her violently. "Tell me! I have no qualms about killing all these people, and taking you away for myself!" There was something niggling him about the woman in his grasp. He peered down at her face, shadowed by the bonnet. He thrust her back. "Take off your hat! Do it!"

Emma regained her composure and slowly untied the ribbons, withdrawing the hat from her head. Her chin raised a fraction of an inch as she watched the recognition dawn in his eyes. Instead of anger, Timmons burst out laughing. It was a horrible sound, sending chills through Emma's form.

"No! It can't be!"

"You came seeking Emmett Hawkins, *sir*. Here he stands or, rather, I stand. We are one and the same."

Something inside his head snapped and Timmons grabbed Emma around the waist, hauling her backwards out of the parlor. Rose cried out as the door slammed against the wall. Emma fought her captor until the cold barrel of the gun met her temple. Her struggles ceased.

"They cannot convict me of anything if you're dead, but there's no reason I can't have a bit of fun first." Timmons reached for the handle of the front door when the sound of a hammer click stopped him.

Colin crouched at the top of the stairs, gun trained on Timmons. The laughing commenced again, harsh and garbled in Emma's ear. His breath reeked of alcohol. "McCafferty! It all makes sense now. I mean, why would a captain care about a lowly private, unless he was actually a she and spreading her pretty little legs for you? Well, I guess I'll get to taste what you did!"

Emma met Colin's stare and he gave her a subtle nod. With all her might, Emma slammed her elbow into Timmons' gut, stamping hard on his instep. She fell forward as he released her, covering her head with her hands as a shot rang out. Colin looked around fearfully, as the bullet had not come from his gun.

Positioned by the foot of the stairs, William drew himself up, the muzzle of his rifle smoking. Timmons fell backwards against the closed door, shock crossing his features as he fell to his knees, gaping down at the blood ballooning onto his shirt. "It wasn't meant to be this way." He collapsed forward, life draining from his body.

Colin raced down the stairs and gathered Emma up into his arms, kissing her repeatedly. She wept openly in his arms. William alerted the family to Emma's safety and urged them to stay in the parlor, for the body of Timmons was not a pretty sight. Colin carried Emma into the parlor, despite her insistences, and rested her on the free settee. Holding out her arms, Rose quickly handed over Anna, who recognized her mother immediately and began to wail to be fed. Using a corner of the baby's blanket for modesty, Emma obliged her daughter immediately.

William set the rifle in the corner of the room and drew his wife to him for a lengthy embrace. Rose leaned back in his arms. "We should check on Millie. I fear that monster has brought harm to her."

Colin moved to the hall, cringing at the body of Timmons in the entry. Millie was coming to and groaned loudly. Gingerly helping her to rise, Colin urged her not to look at the gruesome sight, as he led her to the parlor.

"Mrs. Hastings! She done sent me. Tol' me to git if that there man came back!" Colin handed her a damp cloth to hold against her wound.

William nodded. "Colin and I will go. We will alert the authorities in the meantime." The two men departed, flinging a sheet over the body in the foyer before leaving. When they arrived at the elderly matron's residence, the home was quiet. Colin called out, alerting Mrs. Hastings to the safety of everyone. Upon hearing this, Mrs. Hastings came down the stairs.

"Thank God! I was so fearful! I never knew he would

come here."

William touched her arm. "The man is dead. We do not have to worry anymore. Colin will remain in New York at the hospital and will not be sent back to the front."

"Small blessings! I am so sorry if I have caused your family this distress."

"I believe there is a reason for everything in this world. Without Emma, we might have never known what happened to Harrison. Even though his loss pains me greatly, we have peace."

Rochester, New York
April 9th, 1865

"Rose! Bridget! Will! Emma! Everyone!" William was out of breath as he flung open the door and called out throughout the house.

The family approached from all directions, converging on William in the front entry.

"My lands, what is it?" Rose watched her husband tremble, as he held out the evening edition of the paper.

"It's over! Lee surrendered to Grant at Appomattox Courthouse! The war is over!"

Joyous exultation erupted from the gathered assembly and hugs were eagerly exchanged. Emma's heart soared. The end of the war meant Colin could come home permanently to her and Anna, ready to begin a new life together.

Simple Blessings

A Special Short Story Sequel
to
The Soldier's Secret

This is a work of fiction. Names, characters, places, and incidents are either the product of the author's imagination or used fictitiously and any resemblance to actual people, alive or dead, business, establishments, locales, or events is entirely coincidental.

Any reference to real events, businesses, or organizations is intended to give the fiction a sense of realism and authenticity.

Any errors are the sole responsibility of the author.

Editing by Susie Watson

December 24th 1865
Rochester, New York

The fire crackled merrily in the hearth, as boisterous voices filled the small parlor. Outside the window, snow swirled in an elaborate dance. It was Christmas Eve, the first with the entire Mansfield and McCafferty family under one roof since the start of the war. It was still a somber occasion, having Harrison missing from the fold, but all tried to keep in mind the good that had come of the family's trials.

Wade toddled happily around the Christmas tree, tugging tinsel and colorful balls off. Bridget was always close at hand to replace the objects, before Wade moved on to his next conquest. Anna gleefully babbled on her father's knee, watching the chaos with great joy. Will and Colin both imbibed warm spiced cider, observing the children's antics.

Rose and Emma sat, heads together, speaking of Christmases past, remembering one where Will ended up sledding headfirst into a snow drift. He arrived home with a nose as red as a cherry, and icicles dripping from his wool cap.

Rochester was largely untouched from the ravages of war, aside from the loss of brothers, fathers, and sons. New opportunities had sprung from the tragedies, allowing for greater investments to be made. Factories allowed for quicker production of goods, and the Mansfield family benefited from this through careful investments.

William was returning from such a meeting, hunkered down in his wool coat, seeking the warmth and comfort of hearth and home. He opened the front door to the cozy scene, stomping loose snow off his boots. "Merry Christmas!" his voice boomed through the house. Wade ran, as fast as his young legs could carry him, to his favorite grandparent. He giggled musically as he was hoisted up into the air. "Have you been a good boy for Santa?"

Wade furrowed his small brow. "'Anta?"

William tweaked the small nose, and withdrew a stick of peppermint from his coat pocket. Wade all too eagerly snatched the treat, and into his mouth it went.

"You will spoil him, Papa William," Bridget remarked, as the pair came into the parlor.

Sinking down next to his wife, William laughed, a low, rumbling sound. "What are children for, if not for spoiling?" Wade wriggled away, and went to show his father the treat. "Why, when I was a child, we only got candy once a year. Maple, if I remember. It melted so smoothly in your mouth. Was worth the wait to Christmas."

Emma met Colin's gaze across the family. Both remembered fondly a Christmas spent without family, but in happy company. Ol' Tim had sheltered them well for those five months. They had spoken many times, in private, about the people who had aided their journey, but rarely to the family. The memories were difficult for Rose, knowing her youngest lay buried in those mountains. However, perhaps now was the appropriate time to recollect the kindly man.

"Emma and I were sheltered by a man for a few months in the Appalachians." Colin watched for signs of pain to cross Rose's face, but she seemed intrigued, having heard so little of their trials. "He was a very generous man, and asked us to call him, 'Ol' Tim.' He had run away from a plantation as a young man, seeking refuge in the mountains."

"We came across his cabin, and he invited us to stay. The winter months were hard, with long, daily treks to get enough wood for the fire. Sometimes, the snow was nearly past our heads. We made pathways through it, to get to the woodpile. Often, we were completely exhausted by evening. However, there was plenty of food, and the cabin was safe and warm.

"On Christmas morning, Ol' Tim presented us with a carved cradle. He had worked on it in secret, and his face was the picture of pride presenting it to us. I only wish we could have taken it along. I will always remember his kindness in a savage world."

Emma nodded approvingly, eyes misting at the memories. "Yes, as will I. If not for him, our dear Anna might not be here."

Rose embraced her daughter. "We must never forget the kindness of those who helped when they did not have to."

William, disheartened by the conversation, rose and walked to the hearth, leaning on the mantle. "I have some encouraging news. Benjamin's family has been moved into a small cottage on the edge of town. Thanks to my investments, I've been able to take his mother on as a clerk in the store, while maintaining Benjamin's services. His sister is going to attend the local school."

The mood in the room instantly lightened. "Papa, that is wonderful! How kind of you to do that for Ben." Emma stood, and quickly embraced her father.

William patted her lightly on the back. "'Tis the season for giving back to those who have helped us. I wanted to do it sooner, but the cottage has only just become available. You should have seen the state of the place they were living in. Now, they will have a clean, warm home."

"Dinner, sir, ma'am," one of the remaining servants called out to the family from the door. She would soon be departing for Christmas with her own family, leaving the Mansfield-McCafferty clan to fend for themselves the following day. They did not mind, of course, happy to see their paid staff content. Emma had been flexing her cooking skills, and Rose was not without her own talents. Together, the women would prepare a Christmas feast.

The meal that evening was simple, but no less appreciated. Conversation rose and fell like waves, as pauses were taken to enjoy the taste of the smoked ham and potatoes, with sweetcorn. Never one to leave out the younger members, defying convention, the children ate alongside their parents. As the meal came to a conclusion, a resounding knock on the door reverberated throughout the interior of the cozy home.

"I'll get it. No need to disturb the staff." Colin pushed back his chair, rising from the table. Conversation resumed, as the party awaited news of who had arrived at their door on Christmas Eve.

They could hear hushed murmurs from the entryway, and finally, Colin returned, alone. "Emma, will you come with me please, my love?"

Emma placed her cloth napkin aside, frowning worriedly at her family, before rising and following her husband. He slipped his hand around her waist. "Who is it...?" Her voice caught in her throat as she observed the elderly man at their door. There was no mistaking his relation to her husband.

"Father, this is my wife, Emma," Colin stiffly made the introductions, and Emma could feel the tension in his fingertips.

Emma bobbed a quick curtsey. "Mr. McCafferty."

The man before her bore wrinkles around his eyes, Colin's eyes. He walked with an ebony cane, and the shoulders of his wool coat were dusted with snow. He doffed his hat, bowing his head. "Emma, it is certainly a pleasure to meet you. I apologize for interrupting your family's meal."

The need to be hospitable surged in Emma, and she stepped forward, motioning for the man to come into the parlor by the fire. She took his coat and hat, setting them in a warm place to dry. Colin maintained his position by the door, staring at the parent with whom he had had little contact over the previous years. He had never imagined his invitation to spend Christmas with his new family would be accepted, as he had received no reply.

"Mr. McCafferty, may I get you some coffee? You must be chilled to the bone," Emma, again, broke the uneasy tension between father and son.

He lowered himself onto one of the couches, smiling gratefully. "That would be lovely, my dear. Please, call me

Rian." She could hear a long-forgotten, Irish lilt in his voice, almost faded with time.

Emma placed a gentle kiss on Colin's cheek as she passed, her breath soft against his skin. "I will be back in a moment." She gave him a subtle push forward, and scurried off to report the events to her family.

Colin stepped forward into the room, feeling much like he did as a child, when called up on bad behavior, or poor marks in school. "Father, it's good to see you."

Rian motioned to an empty chair. "Sit, boy. You look nigh close to collapsing! Surprised to see your old man?"

"Very much, sir. I did not expect you to respond to my invitation."

"The snows were pretty thick this year. By the time I received your letter, there was no time to send a suitable response. So, I decided to come myself. I hope I'm not intruding?" Rian's eyes twinkled. He had been estranged from Colin for a few years now, but the pride at seeing his son so well-settled brought great joy to the old man.

Emma returned, followed by Rose. Rian got to his feet, bowing low to the pair. "I have never been served by finer ladies in my life." The Irish charm was quick to his tongue.

The ladies laughed, and Emma placed the tray down. "We thought it best not to bombard you with my entire family at once, but my mother, Rose, insisted."

"An extreme pleasure." Rian took Rose's hand, and kissed it gallantly. Rose shook her head with a laugh.

"You Irish men! Don't think I'm fooled for one minute. I better get back to my husband, and the rest of the family. Emma, why don't you come get Anna?" The pair again withdrew from the parlor, leaving the men in silence.

Rian sat again, resting his hands on his cane. Colin sat as well, secretly hoping Emma returned with haste. He answered the earlier question, "No, you are not intruding. I just never mentioned it to anyone, so they are undoubtedly curious."

"I can see that. Tell me, who is Anna?"

Colin realized he had never mentioned his daughter in the letters, hoping to make the introduction when, and if, his father accepted. "Anna is our daughter."

The cane nearly slipped from Rian's hands. He had recognized the name, but never fathomed it could belong to his granddaughter. His voice caught in his throat. "After your mother?" The memory of his lost wife flooded his mind. He had blamed the boy for her death, but in his later years, realized the error of his ways.

"Yes, Father."

Tears pricked at the back of the old man's eyes. "A suiting tribute. I will admit, I have been unfair to you, Colin. I should have been a better parent while you were growing up."

The muscles along Colin's jaw tensed. These were words he had wanted to hear for his entire life. "You had your reasons, sir."

"No, it was unfair, and I will no longer deny it. I followed your progress the best I could, son. I am so very proud of you, how you went off to serve our country. I made sure I got the papers as often as possible, and held my breath when I came close to where your name would be if..." he trailed off, coughing. "Well, let's just say I'm happy you made it."

Emma returned, cradling her sleeping daughter. Anna's cheeks were rosy from the excitement, and she contentedly sucked her fingers. Colin stood, taking his daughter from Emma, and sitting at his father's side. Emma smiled at the trio, watching Rian dotingly look upon his only grandchild.

"She..." Words failed him. He brushed his fingers over the fine hairs on Anna's head, admiring the small child in silent awe.

Colin's tough exterior melted. The country after the Civil War was full of poverty, mourning, and loss. He had an opportunity to mend a broken relationship, and he knew how lucky he was to have a family to come home to. "She looks like Mother?" Colin had no memories of the woman who had brought him into the world.

Rian coughed, trying to maintain some semblance of composure. "Yes, son, she does. Your mother was a kind, gentle woman, not really suited to living up north during the harsh winters. When she died, she held you in her arms, and made me promise to look after you. I was too stubborn in my grief." Clapping Colin on the back, Rian pushed past years of unspent grief. "I'm sorry, son. I hope you'll let me be in Anna's life, as her grandfather."

Emma burst with pride. "Two doting grandfathers? Anna will hardly want for anything. Please, Rian, will you come into the dining room and meet the rest of my, our, family?"

Rian pushed himself to his feet. "Nothing would please me more, Emma."

Emma linked arms with the elder man, glancing back at Colin.

"I'll stay here a few moments, Emma."

Knowing how much Colin loved to walk Anna around the parlor, Emma nodded, guiding her father-in-law in to meet the Mansfield hoard.

Colin listened with joy as the voices rose up, heard even in the quiet of the parlor. He hoped, after being without anyone for so long, his father would meld in seamlessly with the welcoming Mansfields. He gazed down at Anna, her small chest rising and falling in peaceful slumber. "Well, little one, you certainly are a lucky girl this Christmas." He stood, pacing the room. "You'll never want for a mother or a father, and you will grow up so very loved."

The storm outside the window settled into white blanket, lights flickering from every window. In his low baritone, Colin sang softly to his daughter, watching a small smile set in on her dainty features. Leaving the parlor, he climbed the stairs, grinning at the sound of his father's lilting voice telling an old Irish fable. Laughter followed him up, until he reached the nursery where Wade and Anna slept.

Placing Anna in her bassinet by the window, Colin peered out again, frowning as a shadowy figure crossed the back of the yard, behind the shed. He blinked again, and it was gone. Reminding himself to make sure all the latches were fastened, Colin kissed his sleeping daughter and returned to the dining room, eagerly anticipating a relationship with the man he so longed to know as his father, in the truest sense of the word.

Sunlight glistened through the curtains on Christmas morning. Colin had long forgotten the figure in the back garden, instead longing to see the children's faces when they opened their presents. He especially longed to see Emma's face, when she unwrapped her present. Rian had graciously accepted the invitation to stay the night, pleased beyond recognition to be in the bosom of such a kind, loving family.

After a hearty breakfast, cooked by Rose and Emma, they all descended into the parlor. Emma was beyond thrilled with her new books and fur-lined gloves, as well as a newly engraved wedding ring, professing Colin's never-ending love. Anna drooled and cooed on her new rag doll. Wade shrieked with delight at the wooden toys and sled. Will frowned for a moment, thinking about how hard it would be to trudge up the hill and back with his son.

Recognizing the pain in his son's eyes, William thought it the best moment to reveal his gift. He drew the attention of all those assembled, "Ahem. Now, on my recent business trip, I came across something. In truth, I am amazed with the advances made in this area of medicine." He pulled out a rectangular box, and handed it to his son. "I hope this makes your life a bit more comfortable, Will."

Will's brow creased as he pulled the ribbon off the box, and opened it. Inside, nestled in layers of newspaper, was a perfectly formed wooden leg, leather straps dangling off the back to allow the leg to fit smugly. Tears unabashedly flowed down Will's cheeks. Bridget pressed a hand to her mouth. William harrumphed with pride, as Rose came to his side, hugging him tightly with joy.

Colin passed Anna to Emma, walking over to Will. "May I help you? We can go into the study." He knew the man's pride prevented anyone, aside from Colin and Bridget, to see his wound. Will merely nodded, hoisting his crutch, and leaving the room with Colin carrying the box.

In the quiet of the study, Will sat in his father's chair, rolling his pants leg up. His wound had healed well, considering how some men during the war had been more likely to perish from infection rather than the initial amputation. He bit his lip, looking worriedly at Colin. "Think this will work?"

Colin nodded. "If measured accurately, and made to fit the man wearing it, I don't see why not. Your father was very ingenious in his procurement of this particular prosthesis. I will admit a small hand in preparing the surprise. Now, you must wrap the upper leg in cloth, to prevent blistering. I only really advise wearing it minimally at first." Colin performed the necessary task, strapping the prosthesis on with the leather buckles, and fitting a shoe onto the wooden foot.

Will pressed his lips together, staring at the foreign limb. "I'm not sure about this, Col. You think it'll work? What if it breaks? What if I can't walk?"

"Only one way to find out." Colin held out his hands, and Will grabbed his forearms, gingerly placing pressure on the leg. He was surprised to see it hold his weight. "Put your arm around my shoulders, Will. Just for balance." The men circled the room several times, each time with Will gaining more confidence.

"I think I'm ready."

Taking it one step at a time, Colin close at hand, just in case, Will moved back down to the parlor, stopping in the doorway. Bridget gasped, sending the room into a hushed awe. With careful movements, Will crossed to his wife, his gait still exhibiting a small limp, as he got used to the new leg. "Well?"

Bridget began to laugh and cry, all at the same time. Will pulled her close, kissing her soundly, much to the delight of the gathered family. Bridget blushed to the tips of her curls. "Will Mansfield!"

Too happy to notice the niggling pain from the foreign sensation, Will kissed the tip of his wife's nose. "I cannot wait to take you dancing again, Mrs. Mansfield! In the meantime, I think I do need to sit." Bridget helped her husband back to his seat.

Rian stood, raising a glass of mulled cider. "I want to thank this lovely family for welcoming me with open arms. When I lost my Anna, I never dreamed I could be happy again. Seeing all of you, together, warms my heart."

"Hear, hear!" William agreed, shaking hands with Rian. "We are indeed blessed to have almost everyone alive and well, when so many are not."

As if on cue, the family bowed their heads, sending up thoughts and prayers to those who were without. Rose wiped away a single tear for their youngest son, Harrison, who had been lost at the hands of a vicious Union officer. Wade ended the solemn tribute with a squeal, tired of all the seriousness. He wanted to play! Will obliged, allowing Bridget to help him bundle up to take Wade out in the backyard. Colin joined the pair, at that moment remembering the strange shadow from the previous night. He gave no indication of his worries, as he joined Will with his son.

A boot and oil cloth protected the wooden leg, allowing Will to chase after his son, fighting the pain. Colin warned him gently to take it easy, but he couldn't stop the man from fulfilling his dream of playing with his boy. Colin circled the yard, looking for signs of the intruder. Any footprints had been filled in with fresh snow, yet he found one, pressed into the ground below the overhang of the garden shed.

A clattering in the shed drew his attention. "Will!"

Will moved as quickly as he could to Colin's side. "What is it?"

"I think there's someone in the shed."

Will frantically looked back at Wade, who was padding snow into a ball. "I need to..."

"Yes, yes, go," Colin murmured back in hushed tones, "Send your father out, would you?"

Treading through the snow, Will scooped up Wade. He knew he would be sore come the morning, but it was all worth it. Now, he was worried about what his brother-in-law had heard, making his way back to the parlor.

Colin waited outside the shed door, listening. All sounds of movement had stopped, and he could hear heavy breathing, ending in low sobs. William burst out the back door, rifle in hand. Colin pressed a finger to his lips, moving around to the shed door. William stood poised with the rifle aimed. There was no way he was taking any risks.

Lowering the old, iron latch, Colin creaked the door open. "We're armed. Come out now." His tone was forceful, but calming.

"Captain McCafferty? Sir?" The voice coming from behind some shovels and rakes echoed in the dim light.

Gesturing to William to lower the rifle, Colin called out again, "Yes, I...was Captain McCafferty. It's just Doctor McCafferty now."

A dirt-stained face emerged into the light. The lanky youth wore a tattered Union uniform, threadbare coat, and holey boots. He shivered terribly in the cold. "Sir, do you know Emmett Hawkins? I knew he lived here, sir, but no one knows who I'm askin' about, sir. You knew him though, right?" His teeth chattered with every word.

"Yes, son, I did...do know Emmett Hawkins." Colin smirked slightly back at William, who let out a mighty chuckle, causing the boy to jump.

Colin motioned the youth forward. "Come now. This is

my father-in-law. He means you no harm. Let's go into the kitchen, and get you warm by the fire."

"Thank you kindly, Cap...Doctor McCafferty." The boy tucked his blue-tinged fingers into his pockets, following along after William and Colin.

The kitchen was glowing with warmth, and the boy immediately rushed to the stove, rubbing his hands over the embers.

"I'll go get a drop of whisky for the young man, and let the others know all is well." William removed his hat and coat, leaving the two.

Colin found some bread and handed it to the boy, along with some cold sausages from breakfast. The youth wolfed them down.

"Easy there, son. You'll make yourself sick. When was the last time you ate anything?"

Slowing for a moment, the boy mumbled, "'Round Harrisburg, I suspect, sir."

Colin shook his head. Nearly a week without food. "Did you walk here?"

"Hitched rides where I could, sir. I needed to find Emmett...Private Hawkins, sir. I hope I'm not too late."

"What's your name?"

"Rawlings, sir. Billy Rawlings."

Colin's brow furrowed, recognizing the name of the boy lost in the Rappahannock River crossing during the war. Emma told him about the letter she wrote home to the boy's family. "I remember you. You were reported missing, presumed dead."

Wiping the breadcrumbs away with a hand, Billy nodded. "I thought I was, sir. The river was mighty cold. I washed up on shore, sir. Lucky to be alive when there were bodies floatin' around me." He looked down in shame, red color creeping back into his neck. "I ran. I couldn't do it anymore. I hid out, almost gettin' caught by them patrols. I remember Em sayin' he had family in Rochester. So I knew if I came here, maybe I could find him."

Colin leaned against a countertop, crossing his arms. So many men had fled during the war, and he couldn't say he blamed them. Hell, even he was classed as a deserter at one point, although he was later absolved of any wrongdoing, thanks to Timmons and his spying. "Billy, there's something you should know about Emmett Hawkins..."

"He's dead? Not surprised, sir, if that's the case." Billy appeared crestfallen, despite trying to keep up the tough façade.

Colin chuckled, earning a scowl from the youth. "Not exactly. You see, Emmett Hawkins never really existed, as you know him. Wait here."

Leaving the boy in his state of confusion, Colin went back to the parlor. Eight curious faces met his, even the children interested in the excitement of the holiday. "Emma, there's someone who is here to see you."

"Me? Who could possibly be here to see me? And more to the point, who was in our shed?"

Colin tutted, pressing a finger to her protesting lips. "All shall be revealed, my love. Come with me."

They moved back to the kitchen, the door swinging open, and Emma peering at the boy sitting at the table. Her face slowly morphed into recognition. "Billy?"

Billy sat up, surprised to see a lady addressing him. "Yes, ma'am. That's me."

Colin looped an arm around Emma's waist, drawing her forward. "Billy was hiding in our wood shed, looking for Emmett Hawkins."

Emma gasped, the name she lived with for those troubled years still fresh to her ear. "Emmett Hawkins...you mean, you didn't...?"

"No, I didn't. I leave that to you, my love."

Billy stared at the lady, something very familiar about her eyes. They were kind, reassuring, and...he gasped, unable to form the words. "But...you're his sister?"

Emma shook her head. "No, Billy. I am...was Emmett Hawkins. I disguised myself to find my brothers. I am sorry you were deceived, but I had to help my family."

Billy's face broke out in a giant grin. "Ma'am, you don't have to apologize. I figure no matter what name you went by you still have a good heart."

Sitting opposite him, Emma took his cold hand in hers. "But what about your family? Why did you come here?"

"My family didn't survive the war, ma'am." Billy's eyes filled with tears, and he bit them back with the pride only known to young men. "Your letter, although well-intentioned, broke my ma's heart. Don't be sad though. You couldn't have known I wasn't dead."

Colin's hands cupped Emma's shoulders, and she fixed her eyes on his. "Certainly not, Billy. It was a hard time. People are still suffering from hard times." She patted his hand gently. "Please, stay here as long as you need."

Billy inclined his head. "Thank you kindly, ma'am. I don't want to impose. Just wanted to make sure you knew I was okay, being so good to me and all back then."

"At least get some food in you, and some warmer clothes before you head out again." Emma stood, going off to fetch her mother for help in that very task.

"A bath wouldn't go amiss either." Colin laughed, Billy right along with him.

The following morning, Colin was up early, hearing the chopping of wood coming from the yard. Billy, it seemed, was also an early riser, and attempting to repay the Mansfields for their hospitality. Rose kindly bestowed upon the young boy some old clothes belonging to Harrison. Her reasoning simple, she wanted someone to have use of them, and she knew deep down Harrison would have wanted the same.

Making his way down the stairs, Colin found his father

staring out the kitchen window at the industrious lad. “He certainly is a hard worker,” Rian remarked.

Colin nodded in agreement. “I hope he has little trouble finding employment. So many men coming back from the war have few prospects.”

“It just so happens I have been thinking about that very notion, Colin. Do you think Billy would be willing to come back north with me? I’m not getting any younger, and could do with an apprentice to learn the trade, seeing as you have your practice here.”

Touched by his father’s gesture, and knowing Billy would also provide companionship for the older man, Colin readily agreed to the idea. “It will comfort me to know someone is there to keep you company.”

Rian wrapped his son in a clumsy hug. “I know I wasn’t there for you, boy, but maybe I can give that lad a second chance at a family.”

Holding his father at arms’ length, Colin grinned. “Now that is a fine idea indeed.”

Rian and Billy left the next day, the entire family piling onto the porch to wave goodbye. Emma and Colin hung back, arms around each other. Colin had his father back in his life, and Billy had gained a family, all on one magical day. Glancing up, Colin spotted the mistletoe, hastily tacked to the doorframe by William.

Sweeping Emma into his arms, he kissed her. “Merry Christmas, my love.”

Emma returned his kiss with equal fervor, thankful for each one of the miracles in their lives. “Oh, yes, it certainly has been.”

Historical Note

The American Civil War lasted from 1861 to 1865. It still remains the bloodiest war in American history, with the casualties totaling more than all American deaths in other United States' wars combined. In total, nearly 1,030,000 people died during the conflict.

For more information on the battles and politics of the American Civil War, please consult www.civilwar.org or your local library.

About the Author

Heather Osborne was born and raised in California. She has a Bachelor of Science in Criminology and Victimology, as well as coursework in Early Childhood Education. In 2009, she moved to Scotland. Heather has been writing short stories for as long as she can remember. She also has written and directed several plays. In her spare time, Heather enjoys reading, writing (of course!), theatre, as well as caring for her young son.

If you have enjoyed "The Soldier's Secret," please consider leaving a short review! Thank you!

For more about Heather's books, find her online at: www.heatherosborneauthor.com